To Marie

Simple Faith
Stories from Guatemala

Peace in the Master

Philip Schotzko

Story teller

Philip Schotzko

Illustrations by
Catherine Bertrand, SSND

Sheed & Ward

All Scripture quotes used in this text are taken from the *Good News Bible: Today's English Version*, translated and published by the United Bible Societies.

Sheed & Ward™ is a service of National Catholic Reporter Publishing Company, Inc.

Library of Congress Catalog Card Number: 89-60585

ISBN: 1-55612-265-9

Published by: Sheed & Ward
115 E. Armour Blvd. P.O. Box 419492
Kansas City, MO 64141-6492

To order, call: (800) 333-7373

Contents

Dedicated to
my mother, Marie Schotzko

My Best Teacher
in the ways of
Faith, Hope and Love

Acknowledgements

I wish to acknowledge the support and talents of all those who helped in the writing of these stories. I especially thank Catherine Bertrand, SSND, for her art work and for sharing the joys and sorrows of creation, Bill Huebsch and Paul Goepfert for editors' suggestions, Linda Wanner, SSND, Cathy Huebert and Dorothy Peters for proof-reading and typing, and finally, for the people who lived these stories with me and those that gave me the encouragement I needed to believe in myself as a writer.

Preface

Slowly the thick fog of unconsciousness lifted; I became aware of a sharp edge uncomfortably pressing across my back just below my shoulder blades. Where was I? There was a moment of slight panic: I had awakened in a strange room and could not remember how I had gotten there. Unable to move, I finally forced my eyes open and found myself lying on my back, staring up at the nozzle of a showerhead. The pain across my back was the four inch high threshold that separated the shower from the rest of the bathroom. Bit by bit, my mind began to connect fragmented memories to solve the puzzle of who I was and what had happened:

> Phil Schotzko: Catholic priest . . . 34 years old . . . and very ill. I was at San Lucas Tolimán in Guatemala, checking out the possibility of spending five years here as a missionary. I was in the "Fathers' House," in the bathroom where I had evidently fainted from the effects of amoebic dysentery.

The pain and nausea returned as I regained consciousness, finally forcing me to struggle back to bed to examine the decisions before me: did I really want to go through with becoming a missionary? Was it insane to leave the securities of my home culture, a satisfying position, family and friends, for the unknowns that awaited in San Lucas? Would I be able to endure the sickness and tension of living in a conflict zone where violence from guerrilla warfare is quite common. Would I find a warm place in the hearts of these people?

Concentration was difficult during those long, dark hours of pain; but the questions were urgent. I began reviewing my motivations and assessing my reasons for staying.

First, there was the generally welcoming environment of the parish of San Lucas. For twenty-six years, the Diocese of New Ulm, Minnesota, together with the School Sisters of Notre Dame of the Mankato, Minnesota Province have been committed to the people of San Lucas, sending personnel and financial support to give impetus to an extensive and highly successful Third World development project. The Guatemalans have responded with enthusiasm, gratitude and a generosity of their own. I felt immediately accepted and trusted because of the history of faithful service that I was invited to share.

Secondly, there was the staff of North Americans that I would be working with:

—Father Greg Schaffer, the visionary pastor who offered me the support and affirmation I needed to overcome my fears and who, for a confirmed teacher, showed a remarkable openness to being taught.

—Father John Goggin, the steady maintainer of programs and machines, who has a particular love for the simple plantation workers.

—Sister Linda Wanner, SSND, the educator, especially committed to quality schools, to hospitality and to enjoying life.

—Sister Rose Ann Ficker, SSND, the teacher/mother who poured out her heart to the one hundred or more children in the orphanage.

They seemed to me to be a unique blend of talents and personalities who, together with myself, had the potential of forming an effective ministry team.

Finally, I looked again at my interior motives. I didn't seem to have grand illusions about having the answers or being the savior in the midst of a very complex and difficult ministry setting. I would come with the idea of offering my services in whatever way seemed appropriate, learning what I could from each new situation and returning enriched to my former "mission" in Minnesota.

I also felt a deep down calling that I could not fully understand. There seemed to be an uncomfortable invitation to share the suffering of the poor—and of Jesus—making me adhere to my decision to "give it a try" in Guatemala. In my secure First World life, with all the advantages of a wonderful family, a good education and a respected position, I wondered if I knew enough of the Paschal Mystery from the inside to tell convincingly the "Jesus story."

I chose the less familiar, the less traveled path. I hoped it would lead me to greater detachment from my false securities and to surrender more deeply to the way of a God who became powerless in joining our human culture. Thus, I have spent the past four years entering into the Mystery in a new way. The struggle with a new language, the persistent parasites and viruses that made me sick, the frustrated cries of the poor as well as the wonderful fiestas, new friends and lots of laughter have all been invitations to trust life more than ever. The overriding experience is one of gratitude for the privilege of being called to serve in a cross-cultural setting and to join my life to the lives of the people of San Lucas for this brief time.

One of the results of our time together is this book of stories. As I began to get involved in the daily life-and-death struggles of the Guatemalan people, I found myself touching powerful stories that cried out to be told. The issue was not whether I could tell them well, but that they be heard. I truly believe these stories have their own life and will live on and be retold as pedagogy sees fit.

It should be known that the stories are essentially accurate; some names and places have been changed to protect the innocent—and, in some cases, the guilty. The balance and kinds of stories are of my choosing and reflect my personal experience in Guatemala. It is a land of many paradoxes and contrasts. And in the midst of my own struggle to live beyond my petty fears, I have found it a land and a people that I have grown to love.

Background

The stories in this collection emerge from the unique cultural history and reality of life in the central highlands of Guatemala. A general profile of the social, economic and political situation helps to appreciate some of the subtle nuances in them. I offer the following background to help understand the context and to grasp the significance of these experiences.

Geography:

The parish of San Lucas Tolimán is situated in the department of Sololá on the south shore of Lake Atitlán. This ancient crater lake and its surrounding volcanoes are considered to be one of the most picturesque spots in the world. The jurisdiction of San Lucas is made up of various plantations and villages which are connected by one asphalted road and many rock-strewn, dirt roads that make travel difficult. The mountainous terrain is farmed by hand and, thus, it is able to be semi-forested and agriculturally productive at the same time. Besides the main crops of coffee, corn and beans, there are bountiful flowering plants and trees that accentuate a lush green landscape. The altitude is one mile above sea level. This serves to temper the intense rays of the direct sun and creates average year round temperatures between sixty and eighty degrees. For this reason Gautemala is sometimes referred to as "The Land of Eternal Spring."

People:

The inhabitants of the highlands are divided into two major groups: Indians and non-Indians. The latter called "ladinos" are a mixture of Indian and Spanish ancestry. Besides the language difference between these groups—the ladinos speak Spanish and the Indians one of thirty native languages—there is a vast cultural difference that is the basis for racism and helps ferment a delicate political/economic situation.

The ladinos, who dress in Western clothing, make up the minority—20% in San Lucas—but are economically and educationally the elite who have traditionally dominated the Indians from their position of power. In recent years, however, with increased education and self-confidence, the Indians are coming to appreciate the tremendous cultural wealth contained in their traditions, customs and dress. This adds to the tension between the races and adds fuel to the political turmoil that has become violent in recent years.

Government, Politics and Civil War:

Up until 1985, due to political persecution, both the urban and rural workers had not been allowed to organize and participate in the defense of their cultural, social and political interests. On the other hand, the wealthy sector was well organized and had decisive impact on the economic and political policy, and through an alliance with the army, it placed in power or removed governments at all levels; national, county and municipal. This had been the pattern for thirty years.

Since 1979, a civil war is being waged in Guatemala between groups dissatisfied with existing conditions and the elite in power who are responsible for inhuman exploitation, for thousands of murders, and for corruption in the form of billions of dollars handled by high army and government officials who represent a very small segment of society. The conflict is augmented by leftist political ideologies, but they are not the main cause. The root causes are poverty and its dehumanizing effects.

This civil war among Guatemalans has left a legacy of no less than 150,000 people dead or missing. The war has produced 100,000 orphans and 15,000 widows. Approximately 80,000 Indian peasants have fled to Mexico, in the process losing their lands, homes and few belongings.[1]

Since 1985, Guatemala has entered into a democratic process and ratified a new constitution. The government is beginning to be more responsive to human rights and to allow the lower classes to organize on their own behalf. The political violence has diminished although the fight for the minds and hearts of the common people continues to erupt in various areas, the south side of Lake Atitlán being one of these "war zones."

Religion:

The majority of the inhabitants of San Lucas possess strong spiritual beliefs based in the Mayan Indian culture of their ancestry. The beliefs contribute to making the town rich in the colors of native weavings, in folklore and in religious customs based in the cycles of nature. For example, the blessing of seeds for planting and the thanksgiving offering of the first fruits of the harvest are important rituals.

With the arrival of the Spanish missionaries, the majority of native people began actively to practice the Catholic religion in their communities. The native spirituality was vigorously suppressed in the colonial period but was secretly practiced along side of the Christian faith, resulting in rituals that reveal a mixture of the two belief systems.

In the last fifteen years an intense evangelization campaign by fundamentalist Christian groups has spread throughout Guatemala gaining many converts and causing painful divisions in families and communities.

Economic and Living Situation:

The people of the Sololá/San Lucas region are materially very poor. The average income per family is about $50.00 a month.

Most struggle just to survive from month to month. Malnutrition is the principle cause of sickness and death. 82% of children below the age of five suffer some degree of malnutrition.[2] Information from a 1987 survey taken in the Diocese of Sololá include:

72% of the houses do not have water
82% of the houses do not have electricity
91% of the houses do not have a sewer system
59% of the population do not read or write.[3]

Agriculture provides the basis for the economy. Some are employed as day laborers on the coffee and sugar plantations, others own two or three acres of land on which they raise corn and beans, their main staple foods. There is a problem in that 85% of the arable land of Guatemala is in the hands of the affluent 10% of the population, while the remaining 90% must survive on the yield of 15% of the land.[4] Through land ownership the wealthy consolidate their economic and political power while the peasant farmers are forced to work for an inadequate wage.

Unemployment or under-employment in Guatemala now approaches 50%. This problem along with a high incidence of alcoholism are the major sources of family stress. Nevertheless, family units in the predominantly Indian culture remain intact largely due to the strongly re-enforced male and female roles and the support of the larger extended family.

Stories of Faith

Faith is the interior quality that urges us beyond the in-securities of doubt to firmer ground where we are free to act without fear, handing ourselves over to the paradoxes of life without regret and with tenacious confidence. Some of these stories emerge from traditional, Catholic belief systems, customs and ways of passing on "The Faith." Others are born of the everyday survival struggle of a people who constantly live on the edge of disaster and would quickly slip into the abyss, were it not for their faith. These tales are told with the hope that they will invite us to embrace our God-given human existence with the same abandon with which God embraces us.

A Missing Button

As I remember my childhood, some of the most incredible dramas of my life focused on buttons and zippers, pins and tie strings . . . those all-important things that had to be used properly, according to adult values and, later, peer fads. As I've grown older, my focus on what fastens clothes together has shifted to contemplating what connects people to one another. But in this story I would like to go back to one of those primeval buttons, a real button, that was supposed to help hold together my pants.

I had come to Guatemala with a pair of pants that somehow was missing the button above the zipper. It simply disappeared in the wash one day and now, for several months, I had been making do by locking the zipper securely and tightening my belt over the buttonhole and the adjacent flap. It worked, more or less, but I just couldn't get over the uncomfortable feeling that, when I least expected it, the zipper would sneak down as I stopped to pick up something. This would not be a catastrophe in itself but, unnoticed, it could be rather embarrassing.

So one day I was walking through the kitchen wearing these pants which, in spite of this slight flaw, were one of my favorites. As usual, old Martha was there, and a group of young, giggly Mayan Indian girls who helped with the meals. Now Martha is an interesting woman. The daughter of a "healer," she has hundreds of natural medicinal cures and black hair in two braids that fall over her shoulders. She generally wears a slightly tattered cardigan that is unbuttoned most of the time. She had worked as a cook with the sisters and priests for many years and considered them her family. However, knowing this did not prepare me for what she was about to do.

As I bent to capture a carrot that had escaped from the cutting board I remembered the pants that I was wearing. Self-consciously I took a quick look to make sure all was well. But somewhat tired of the charade, I mentioned to Martha my little problem because sometimes she would do some mending for me. I asked, "Martha, would you happen to know if there is an old button laying around that would work to fix my pants?" Then I indicated the size I might need. I thought every house had a button box, as we did at home, but I've since learned that here buttons, like rags, are a rare and precious commodity.

Martha's response was so quick and I was so startled that I didn't have time to stop her. She whisked a scissors off the table and, without hesitation, snipped off the button and gave it to me. "Here," she said, "you can use the bottom button from my sweater. I never use it."

I could do nothing but thank her sheepishly, turn and walk out, staring at the button in my hand. What was it in her life experience and cultural values that made such a generous response possible? What had shaped me so differently that I was startled?

Suddenly the lines between rich and poor, developed and undeveloped blurred within me as I saw more clearly than before my attachment to things. And I felt connected to Martha as never before.

Baby Wanted

At six o'clock one Sunday afternoon in the far corner of the mission, I fired up the old blue pickup truck. I wanted to hurry home to the warm hearth and friendly supper gathering that make Sunday evenings a delight. A thick, gray cloud of smoke escaped from underneath somewhere but I knew this was normal for "Ol' Blue." That didn't stop me from whispering a plea for providence to ride with us.

A young mother with a sick child in her arms suddenly appeared in the twilight asking for a ride up to the parish clinic. "Of course," I responded, and it was not at all surprising that as the bent door sprang open two other children simply materialized out of nowhere and jumped up beside me like dogs eager for a Sunday drive in the country. Then about a half-dozen teenage boys asked for a lift to the communities up the road. They climbed up in back. So far it was an ordinary experience.

But the ante was raised when we passed by the plantation St. Theresa. We were flagged down by two men heated up from a three mile run from another plantation set back in the mountains and accessible only by a sturdy four-wheel drive vehicle. There was the usual greeting of "Pardon me, Padre," then the news that a woman was seriously sick and needed to be taken to the clinic.

I thought for a minute of the three rivers to cross to the plantation, the not-at-all dependable truck, the sick child I already had with me, and a visiting priest patiently waiting farther down the road for me to pick him up. It was the late hour and the unreliable truck—and perhaps the warm hearth—that cinched it, and I said I would have to first go up and send down a better truck and another driver. They said they would ride along, pressing their petition and ensuring the urgent response that it deserved.

4

After dropping off and picking up others along the winding road, we arrived at the church and clinic, and I showed the mother where to find help for her child.

Next, I ran to get keys to the red Toyota, but they weren't in the drawer, as often happens. Nor were they in my pocket, as also happens when I forget to return them. I ran to Father John's house, knowing he used the truck last. Remembering the tough schedule he had that day, I was reluctant to disturb him; I figured he was trying to catch a half-hour nap before supper. As I approached the house, I picked up a stone to toss on his tin roof to wake him up. I hoped he would not be upset.

Wonder of wonders! The gate was open. He was up and around and quickly found the keys. Now the task was to find a driver who could do this mission of mercy while I joined my friends at the table. After all, I wasn't ordained to be an ambulance driver.

As I pulled out of the driveway, I asked what seemed to be the problem with the woman down in the plantation, though I wasn't sure I wanted to know. When they replied that it was a woman having difficulty giving birth, the ante quickly went up again. I was finally shaken from my "homing" urge, as my imagination began to run wild with all the possible endings to the story I was being dragged into.

Angel, our trusty driver, was not at home. Though another driver was probably available but on the other side of the village across a valley, I said with resignation, "Well, let's go!" I sent one of our volunteers to call the doctor and have him waiting at the clinic when we got back.

The dust flew and chickens scattered as we raced down the twisting mountain road. But as fast as I went, my imagination went faster. I had seen one live birth but certainly was not qualified to do anything but hold a sweaty hand . . . preferably my own. I saw images of a hemorrhaging, unconscious woman. I heard screams and groans and even thought about wrapping a bloody newborn baby in my favorite sports jacket.

We probably would have gotten there in record time except for having to pull over quickly to avoid hitting a man passed out stone drunk in the middle of the road. There was no one in sight so we lifted him to a more comfortable resting place in the ditch and raced off again into the dark night.

Because this particular plantation has no electricity, it was pitch black as we drove up. I could only see the outline of the simple square buildings called houses. I sent the two men to see if they could bring the woman while I turned the truck around. Actually, I was reluctant to go to the house for fear of what I might find. Quite soon, to my great relief, an obviously pregnant woman came walking on her own with a man, presumably her husband, at her side. She looked older than I expected. (It is often the first child of a young teenager that causes problems.) From the gathering of the whole community around her as she shuffled along, I guessed that she was a respected matron.

She groaned and expressed her anxieties and fears. The background voices in a mixture of Spanish and native dialect formed a spontaneous chorus of words of encouragement and pleas for God's help and protection. I marveled at this natural, Christian community reaching out and enveloping this woman and her family in their need.

The ride back was better than I expected; certainly it was slower. There were only occasional groans when I would hit a bump. There was even a bit of conversation—if her husband had jumped in the back of the pickup, if they had other children and, of course, about the poor quality of the road.

Arriving at the clinic I was hoping to hand her over to the competent hands of our native doctor. Dr. Miza had been a carpenter but, seeing the desperate need for better health care for his people, he had asked Father Greg to support him through medical school so he could come back and serve in the parish clinic. He is almost always on call, but, as luck would have it, he was out of town and his assistant had not come yet. Just one untrained nurse was on duty. She casually told the woman to walk right into the examining room as if she were the twenty-third patient of the day in a typical North American doctor's office.

By this time I was beginning to lose my cool! I ran to the priest's house to get help. Father John relieved my anxiety with his lighthearted and experienced comments as he went to check out the situation. He came back smiling confidently that this child would be fine—the mother had already given birth to ten others.

I was not so confident when at midnight I was awakened by the nurse and the doctor's assistant banging on my window. They were requesting the Toyota keys that I had, for once, remembered to return to the drawer. They needed to go to another clinic across town to get some medicine to induce labor again. So the drama continued as I lay awake doing what I could—praying and wondering at the ordinariness of it all, and yet, how extraordinary for me to be part of this story.

In the morning I visited the new mother and her healthy baby boy. She didn't say much, but she looked up at me with tired and proud eyes. The words on her lips were simply, "Thank you, Padre." I wondered what stories surrounded the births, lives and deaths of her other children. Seven out of eleven are still living. About average for Guatemala!

I also talked to the doctor's assistant. He said, with a smile, "There is no reason why that baby wasn't born in the bouncing pickup last night. She was fully dilated when she arrived at the clinic."

I whispered a little prayer of gratitude that Providence had gone with us.

A March of Hope

The first Pentecost must have been wild and wonderful—one of those experiences that makes you say, "I wish I could have seen that with my own eyes." But did you ever wonder if or how that same powerful Spirit is present and active in the world today? There is always so much bad news to report, that I would like to share a little good news that happened in San Lucas on Pentecost a few years ago.

About the middle of Lent I had an idea. It was like a seed—not that unique, new or different from other dreams, but, evidently an idea whose time had come. Since it was the International Year of Peace (against all evidence to the contrary) and since the Good Spirit is the source and impetus toward peace, I thought "On this Pentecost, why not have a huge march for peace and celebrate the birthday of the church?" I imagined the spirit of the gathering to be more of prayerful expectation and festive gratitude than a tight-lipped protest over the violence and wars (personal and political) that we have known.

I checked it out with the rest of the staff and with some of the folks of the parish and almost immediately the seed began cracking open and sprouting through some unseen force. These being people always "on foot" and loving processions and fiestas, they seemed to intuitively grasp the excitement, if not the significance, of such a pilgrimage. To use a Minnesota image, it was like starting a small snowball rolling down a steep hill.

After a few announcements and meetings with the catechists and heads of the various communities in the parish, the dream began to grow and take shape. We would meet five miles down the road from San Lucas in one of the plantations and walk up to the parish center, culminating with a Pentecost liturgy celebrated on the steps of the church, overlooking a courtyard full of shining faces.

8

I was surprised at how easy it was to organize. Without concern for the dangling loose ends, I even took off for Mexico to buy books and see Mexico City the week before Pentecost. When I returned, I was presented with a list of those in charge and their responsibilities. So, I just sat back and let it happen, sensing that something much bigger was now the prime mover.

At the appointed time, exactly 7:30 a.m., which in itself is a miracle by Guatemalan standards, the long line of brightly dressed and excited marchers began to move. Each group carried its own creative banner with symbols and slogans of the Spirit and of peace. There were the charismatics, cursillistas, the youth group, the Catholic Action folks, fraternities, schools, and different plantations and communities—possibly twenty diverse groupings, 2,000 people, strung out for a mile—all marching, singing and praying together on this special day.

Our parish is quite "normal" in that there are competition and, sometimes, caustic criticism among the divergent groups. But this day all conflict seemed to have been set aside. Instead of jockeying for position, they graciously accepted their assigned place in the flow of the masses.

The organization was incredible; from the red flag waver up front, to the waterboys, to the truck drivers who were helping with the transportation, all seemed to have just the right job and were enjoying doing it. For that I can take no credit; it was done while I was in Mexico.

The Mass was a real high, taking me back to other special celebrations of Pentecost, especially that of my Ordination nine years earlier. I truly felt the blessing and power of the Spirit in my heart, but, more importantly, I felt that the Spirit had indeed come to visit us as in the days of old.

As I sit here writing and remembering, I find myself basking again in the afterglow, tasting once more the fruit of a seed to which the Lord gave power to produce a hundredfold. And I am very grateful—grateful for everything except the nest of biting fire ants that didn't like my clumsy foot trampling on their home as I stepped off the road to photograph the colorful procession.

The Teacher Becomes the Taught

I would like to share a graced moment, a surprise, as it turned out, when reality called into question my perception of the way things are and what is important. In this case, my illusion was about what youth find important and inspiring.

I decided one night to pray the rosary with my teenage friends in the San Lucas youth group. The rosary has not been my strong suit of late; in fact, I was lucky to be able to find my beads. They were stuck away in the dusty corner of a seldom-used drawer. How different from when I was at Crosier Seminary and we used to sneak out of study hall to go down into the crypts to "say the rosary." Being in the midst of adolescent limit setting, I doubt that our motivation was purely religious. Perhaps the praying idea was an exercise in easing our consciences. After all, signing out of study hall on the pretext of going to the library couldn't be too serious a sin if you really were stealing off to say the rosary instead.

Anyway, I jumped in the old blue pickup, which, as usual, didn't want to start. But with a little luck I got it going and even found the right house. I was late by "gringo" time but otherwise right on time. I knocked and pushed the door open a little. There were excited greetings of "Padre Felipe," bright faces reflecting candlelight in dark sparkling eyes and warm words of welcome. The 15′ by 12′ living room that doubled as a bedroom at night was already full of about thirty young people, most of them from 15 to 20 years old. They were kneeling on the hard cement floor, facing a corner that contained a home altar with an image of Mary, candles, a picture of Jesus and other simple decorations and religious symbols.

11

As soon as I knelt down they began. I was distracted by their attentiveness, their discipline of body and obvious devotion that was expressed through this traditional prayer form. Each decade had a special intention as well as a Scripture passage and reflection about the nature of the mystery remembered. Watching them took me back to those nights in the crypt when we used to say the rosary, except that we prayed while sprawled out on the carpet or slouched in the corner, to be as comfortable as possible.

They remained kneeling the whole forty minutes and even recited a long (at least to me) litany to the Sacred Heart at the end of the rosary. There were no distracting whispers, no shuffling from one position to another to betray boredom and no complaints about sore knees or back. Mine were killing me, but I didn't dare move. Eventually, I was taken into the gentle rhythm of the prayers—syllables half familiar but still a little mystical.

The surprise came when it was over. I was disappointed. I didn't want it to end. I didn't want to break the spell.

When the words stopped, the kids made their elaborate sign of the cross and kissed their thumb as it formed a cross with their index finger, a gesture which is a part of their signing ritual. Some also kissed the crucifix of the rosary. Then, they bounced up and began to chatter happily as youths do. But not for long, for they had homework to do for school the next day. They had come to pray and that was finished. So, they broke up in little groups of twos and threes and headed for their homes and shacks.

The amazing thought that kept running through my mind was the realization that they come together in this way for the rosary every evening during Lent. I felt very proud of them and humbled as I looked to my own faith expressions. I was even a bit sad, as I realized how often self-indulgence and lack of discipline rob me of some of the choicest fruits of faith.

The Valiant Women of Guatemala

This is not just one story of faith; it is a story multiplied hundreds, even thousands of times across the face of Guatemala. After the violence, with half the nation unemployed and alcoholism rampant, it is the women who are left to pull the family together and carry on. And they do . . . often against all odds.

There's Martha who, with one child in her womb and another on her back, worked full days in the field with hoe and machete to feed herself and her three children after her husband and father were murdered . . . Or Rose who, with her four girls, endures the periodic abuse of her frustrated and drunken husband . . . Like the grandmothers and aunts who have taken in some of the more than 100,000 civil war orphans of Guatemala, they struggle to clothe, feed and raise their children and maintain their dignity.

These women present me with a noble image of fidelity. Their work is unbelievably hard. They rise at four or five every morning to start the fire, grind the corn by hand, carry water and collect firewood. Always surrounded by two to four children, they move in family units to and from the market, the clinic, the lake, or the fields. Some of these places are important social gatherings and they can be seen chatting pleasantly with other women as they wash clothes at the lakeside or patiently await their turn in line for the doctor.

I have never seen so many beautiful women. Many of our visitors have noticed it, too . . . a unique kind of beauty that defies description. Their faces are creased from strong rays of the sun or blotched because of poor nutrition. So many are missing teeth. They have work-worn hands with dirty fingernails. They are all dressed in the same peasant uniform. Often their woven

13

blouses and wrap-around skirts are frayed or faded and the children in their arms have such smeared faces they almost look like clowns. Yet, they are so beautiful.

Perhaps it is the valiant struggle they live out day to day that fills in the cosmetic flaws. Perhaps it is the warm yet shy glow with which they look at the Padre. Perhaps it is their patient acceptance of life as it unfolds for them, an attitude akin to Mary's "Let it be." I don't know exactly, but they are attractive. They seem to understand who they are and are proud to be women. They lead me to wonder: would I rather be an Indian man or a woman in Highlands Guatemala?

I'm not sure. I do know that I am deeply grateful for the privilege of serving as a priest among them. I especially long for the chance to hear more of the stories of these remarkable women in a setting that is a mutual sharing between equals, and not the usual story of hard times and desperate, present need.

Bless them, Lord, and bless their children. May they always be free to offer life and hope through the cultural expressions that strengthen their identity as women.

Virgin and Mother

One day in May, a delegation from the youth group crowded around my door. They wanted to help build a Marian grotto that would be the focus for their rosary devotion. I was impressed by their devotion to Mary and appreciated their ideas and initiative. Thus began this story of the creation and dedication of a special statue in the corner of the church garden. It is a story colored by my own humanness and the goodness of God.

Since Father Greg and I already talked about transforming the dusty parking lot beside the church plaza into a flower garden, the stone work for the flower beds, fence and grotto wall was soon begun.

More difficult was the search for the statue itself. I had noticed that the traditional statues of Mary in every Catholic Church and most homes in Guatemala are usually of Mary alone—tall, light skinned and dressed in blue and white. In these statues and in the devotion of the people she stands as the *glorious virgin,* somewhat beyond their human experience, almost a goddess. Also, I began to notice many statues of mothers in the central parks of many villages. These images honoring *motherhood* were always "with child" revealing the deep respect that this culture holds for the role of woman as mother. But nowhere did I find a work of art that attempted to bring together the two strong values of "Virgin Mary" and "Motherhood." I wondered how it could be done and whether it would be appreciated.

After talking with many people, I decided to give it a try. I first chose two young Indian mothers who, with their babies, were willing to be photographed as models for the statue. Then, excited by how the pictures turned out, I went to the capital to search for the best sculptor to create the work of art.

15

This was very difficult because I knew no artists nor the process of commissioning a work of art. I had to return several times before the search for the virgin/mother artist was successful. Finally, after six months I was called in to view the clay image that would be used to make the mold for the final form. I was delighted by what I saw. We made only a few adjustments to bring out the typical qualities of San Lucas Indian clothing.

Within a month I brought to the parish the white, marble dust statue of the virgin and child. The mother with Indian features had a crown of stars and the boy had a little hat that almost looked like a halo. The effect was stunning. I hoped the people would be able to say, "Here is one of us who became all she could be."

One of our teachers had advised me to select carefully the day of blessing and inauguration for the image. He said it would make a difference in how the statue was received. The Indian people who had previewed it seemed to like it, but I was concerned about the small but influential group of non-Indian women who are the "keepers" of the Marian customs in the parish. Their response was more politely positive than sincerely enthusiastic. I sensed that here was a situation where the prejudice of racism, usually hidden below the surface, could boil into open conflict. However, they did agree to help with the preparations for the dedication on Sunday, May 31, the Feast of the Visitation.

The day before the feast brought a hint of the testing that was to come. The construction work of the base and roof for the statue was not completed with enough time to clean up and decorate. In fact, even with my anxious presence pushing them along it never quite got finished. And when I returned from a Mass that evening, I found the workers all gone for the weekend and the garden area still a mess. I felt very alone as I tried to pick up the garbage and prepare for the celebration. I wondered if I had made a mistake. Did anyone besides myself feel committed to this project? I consoled myself thinking that at least the Marian women had promised to help decorate early the next morning and the youth group was preparing to dramatize the gospel of the Visitation.

But the next day, I was even more disheartened and, eventually, angry. It was truly Sunday—a day of rest. No one seemed to be able to lift a finger unless directly asked to do so and having the Mass outside by the grotto took a lot of setting up. The sculptor and his family came and I had planned to have a nice meal for them, but they wanted to leave immediately after Mass. Another disappointment was that one of the models didn't want to come because of shyness, and the other didn't show up until halfway through the Mass.

The ladies didn't show up to help decorate until fifteen minutes before the Mass and by that time I was running around in circles and my stomach was doing flip-flops. Eventually, they approached as a group to ask if they could bring out their traditional virgin statue and set it beside the altar during the Mass of dedication. With great control and patience I explained that with the artist present we wanted to keep the focus on the new image and emphasize its unique qualities. They left obviously unconvinced and cornered me once more in the sacristy as I was trying to recollect myself. This time the most determined among them stepped forward and insisted on having another Mass to start off their usual procession and to bless their statue!

That was when I lost my temper. I responded angrily, "There will be no extra Mass. I will bless your statue at the regular 5 p.m. Mass. And don't bother me any more." I cooled down enough to begin Mass and, in spite of problems with the wind and the microphones, it was a beautiful celebration. But on the inside I was in turmoil. I spent much of the afternoon regretting my angry words and wondering how I was going to make peace with the ladies.

I decided that I would have to put liturgical principles aside for the moment. At the five o'clock Mass, the Sunday readings and their corresponding theme should have taken precedence but it became a full blown Marian Feast—homily and all. And at the end, I had an elaborate blessing ritual of their virgin. As I greeted them at the exit, I apologized and asked for their forgiveness. While acknowledging the hurt, they were forgiving. One of them whispered that while I was practically drowning their image in holy water, her friend had turned to her and said, "Now Padre Felipe is forgiven." I was relieved and grateful that it was all over.

Now, every night as I pass the virgin/mother glowing under a flood lamp, I am warmed by the memories it evokes of the strange circumstances that God uses to communicate love and mercy. Somehow through our humanity, just as through Mary's, God's plan will save and we can only rejoice.

Holy Week

This is the story of Semana Santa *(Holy Week), a story that is retold every year in Guatemala. Each village has unique customs but emphasis is placed on the high holy days of* Holy Thursday, Holy Friday, *and* Glorious Saturday, *as they are called here.*

During my first Holy Week in San Lucas, I was filled with the involving wonder of a child, but, at the same time, I felt like a tourist, an outsider, trying to capture and preserve it all on film. Being a celebrant for the formal church liturgies helped me bridge the gap and take an active part in the special pageantry of these days.

Holy Thursday

Thursday was the day of washing feet and it was not just a symbolic washing. It became instantly clear why the custom was so important in Jesus' time and why his action at the Last Supper spoke so powerfully to his disciples.

In the totally Indian community of *Cerro de Oro* (Hill of Gold) a rough wooden table was set in the middle aisle of the church. There were benches on the sides for the "apostles" and a chair on the end for me, the celebrant. After the homily, surrounded by the community singing their hearts out, we were served sweet bread and a hot chocolate drink. We ate in silence. Then I was handed a towel and a clay water jar—the same kind that the women use every day to carry water from the lake. One by one the elders of the community in their native dress came forward, slipped off their sandals and offered their dusty feet to be washed. As I wiped them dry and somewhat cleaner, I would look up into their dark, weathered faces and see in their eyes a deep and subtle glimmer of appreciation. When I had finished with "The Twelve," the towel was almost black and in the bottom of the basin that was used to catch the water there was a thick layer of silt.

My own identity seemed to merge as never before with the power and action of the Lord. (I could have been in Galilee or Jerusalem with Jesus and the apostles.) We were there—or they were here. *They* are *We!*

Holy Friday

All of Holy Week is a holiday for the people of Guatemala, but Friday is the climax of the pageantry in terms of the number of people who gather to participate in the processions. They come together with a spirit that combines picnics on the Fourth of July, the commercial games and vendors of the county fair and the devotional services and processions more common in the 1950s. Most of the day there are hundreds of folks milling around in front of the church or crowding inside when the life-size image of Jesus is hung on the cross at twelve o'clock noon. The arms of this statue are movable so that when he is taken down, exactly at three p.m., the arms are folded at his side and the "body" is laid in a glass casket.

From five in the afternoon until two o'clock in the morning, the casket is placed on an elaborately decorated platform and carried in shifts by thirty men at a time. Then slowly, so slowly, they inch their way through the stone and dirt streets under the festive arches that were built and decorated the night before, and over intricate carpets of flower petals and brilliantly colored sawdust. Each family or community group designs and lays the carpet before the approaching procession. The shuffling feet of the carriers mix the colors and quickly all becomes a strange conglomeration of sand, sawdust and trampled petals.

I was amazed at the way the people express their faith through these rituals and customs. For example, as the crowd surged forward to reverence the cross with the corpus on it, I observed one young girl who had helped carry the statue of Mary in procession. She herself became transformed into a beautiful image of Mary weeping at the foot of the cross. Her eyes, glistening with tears, were riveted on the image of the suffering Christ. Her lips murmured half audible prayers of sorrow and penitence. She was one among the hundreds to place their offerings, their candles and their kisses before the Clown of God who died a fool's death in the eyes of worldly wisdom.

Especially on this day I felt like a tourist—outside of their experience of close identification with the passion of Jesus. I truly was an observer because most of the traditions are carried on without the initiative or organization of the priests or the other parish staff. It is the people's unique faith expression and I was like a visitor invited to play a small part. I began to wonder about the unique religious history of Guatemala that has made these people the carriers of their own ritualized expressions of faith, while, so often, parishioners in the United States just show up as the priest performs the ritual.

Glorious Saturday/Easter

After staying up the night before to witness the processions, I slept late, then worked on my Easter homily. After lunch I went to the beach for a swim and to picnic with 85 children from the orphanage. I was reminded of a personal rule of thumb that I used while guiding canoe trips which says that twelve kids around one campfire is *more than enough*. Nevertheless, I did enjoy just being with them, especially because I didn't have to worry about the details.

Later, I celebrated one Easter Vigil service in a plantation. It was an exercise in frustration because the people were in a wildly festive mood and not ready to reflect on the Easter mysteries. There had been little planning and too few had a sense of what was happening.

The real Easter celebration for me began at dawn. Rising at 4:30, three visitors and I squeezed into a small pickup and headed for Cerro de Oro. They rang the bell as we drove up in the dark. Few were up yet, but soon they were drifting in. We began in the courtyard with the lighting and blessing of the Easter fire and Christ candle. Processing into church we proclaimed the *Exultet*, the formal announcement of the Easter mystery and its significance.

Then the whole community climbed a rugged hill that overlooks the village and gives a breath-taking view of beautiful Lake Atitlán, with its surrounding volcanic mountains. The way up was steep and people had to help each other along, especially those with babies needed a hand now and then. Once on top, in an area cleared for a new church, we began the Easter Mass.

The sun peeked over the mountain across the lake just as the Gospel of the Resurrection was being proclaimed. No matter that it was in their native tongue and I didn't understand a word; its power was obvious in the faith/action of this basic Christian community. In the end, we had a special blessing for that holy place which will house their dreams in the form of a unique church that befits their strength as a faith community.

I have celebrated many Masses in extraordinary settings but this one stands out as somehow reliving, in a special way, the Last Supper, the Sermon on the Mount, and the Crucifixion/Resurrection/Ascension all rolled into one.

The Fiesta of St. Joseph

I would like to tell you about a community celebration that I enjoyed on March 19th, the Feast of St. Joseph. There is a little village of about eight hundred people just a few kilometers down the road from San Lucas that celebrates that day as their patronal feast. That calls for a week of *fiesta* which excludes normal work and includes music, dancing, buying what you can't afford and often drinking what you can't handle. But for the faithful church community of this village, it means preparing for and celebrating the sacred customs and sacraments with appropriate devotion.

I had been warned that this year was going to be *muy alegre* (very exciting) with fifteen First Holy Communions and a dozen weddings all at one time. My mind raced ahead to the logistical problem of organizing the general chaos that can engulf such a ceremony. I recalled with joy and trembling the one hundred and fifteen baptisms that I had celebrated four months earlier in Santiago. My fears were tempered, however, as I also remembered the twenty-five dedicated and talented catechists who are a part of that faith community. They would have instructed everyone in the significance of sacraments to be received, and how to celebrate them with reverence and order.

The fifteen little ones had been meeting three times a week for months, learning about Jesus in the Eucharist. They marched in perfect order dressed in new or clean clothes with a rosary around their neck and a burning candle in their tiny hands. There was some confusion as to whether they should all sit on one side of the church, but that was solved by overruling the Padre who obviously was not at the practice.

Next came the twelve couples, all Guatemalan Indians. The couples were surprisingly young, because in many of these traditional communities, they do not marry in the Church until they have been "joined" for a few years. The women wore variously colored, woven or embroidered blouses along with their new wrap-around skirts. Each had a long white veil hanging down her back and tucked under her chin, so that shiny brown cheeks and black eyes contrasted with the white framing them. The men sported crisp new shirts and they, along with their spouses, carried a candle and a single yellow flower.

They walked solemnly in order but chaos had the upper hand for sometime as they tried to squeeze into the allotted space on the rough wooden benches. Eventually we were able to begin. Their usually serious faces in such a formal setting were transformed as singing filled that little wooden church. The rest of the community could not fit inside so, as always, they had to stick a speaker out the hole in the back wall so all could at least hear what was going on.

The ritual is quite similar to what is familiar to American Catholics. But instead of lighting a unity candle, an unending chain is wrapped around each couple. Another tradition here is the giving and receiving of coins as a sign of the material sharing that will be necessary to provide for the family. This exchange is also an affirmation of the traditional male and female roles that gives stability to family life in this culture.

What struck me this time was the communal nature of the celebration. Just belonging to this group of people—praying and promising their love to each other in the midst of the whole village was more important than "doing their own thing" with a unique, individual ceremony. Afterward, the whole village processed to an area where a temporary shelter from the sun had been erected. The special food shared with delight and gratitude was sweet bread and hot chocolate.

It is times like these that make me so thankful for the opportunity to serve here in San Lucas. They also make me aware of some of the urgent needs that cry out to be heard . . . in this case, for an adequate church building and gathering hall. They have dreamed for eight years of having a real church and not the tin-roofed shack that is less than half the needed size.

Their dreams will not be in vain. If all goes well, within a few months, we will break ground and, stone by stone, raise a building to match their faith.

An Inner Journey

I would like to share a different kind of story, trusting that a small insight into someone's interior world might be as universally touching as a big event. I will try to reveal some of my spiritual journey, including an eight-day retreat that I had the good fortune, or "grace," to experience after Easter.

It had been almost two years since the last retreat and, for me, that is a long time! At least once a year since high school I have looked forward to and come to depend on a special time of reflection and prayer. It is not spiritual pulse taking—at least not anymore—but a time to remember more clearly who God is, who I am and how very "lucky" or blessed I am by a loving "Father." Having lost my flesh and blood father at age fourteen, this is very important to me.

Ministry in a cross-cultural setting has its particular challenges, but the built-in insecurities of living as a stranger in a strange land intensify some of my fears: fear of failure in ministry, fear of being misunderstood, fear of abandonment, and fear of losing control. In the face of these fears I have tried to keep things in perspective through writing in a journal and, in recent months, have begun to use a very simple prayer form called "The Jesus Prayer," which is prayer of the heart. It is the simple repetition of the phrase "Jesus, Son of God, mercy." It helps to dispel my fears and remain at rest in the flow of the Spirit. Nevertheless, I had often found myself struggling against the current and, thus, I was looking forward to a time just to be with God and the goodness of creation.

The first day of retreat, after being encouraged to "ask big," I put into words the desire of my heart: "Lord, I want to be shown the way into your *heart* and there to *know* and *be known* in *love* and *truth*. I would like to learn some keys to open permanently the doors that lock me in on myself and away from you . . . ways

26

to pray always and stay centered; ways to love tenderly without clinging; and ways to act justly, going beyond my fears to wise compassion."

In those first days it became clear that at times I have lived under the illusion that I can be so good and successful that God and others would surely have to love me. While the other side of the same coin (and one of my fears) says, "I could be so bad that God and my friends would reject me and withdraw their love from me." What a joke! Actually, it is a point of pride that anyone could consider themselves so important or powerful as to manipulate God or even the best of human love.

I found myself restless, striving so hard to be "strong, loving and wise" (2 Timothy 1:6 ff). I tried to imitate my mentors that I might *be known* as holy and wise. How vain to presume that I could make myself holy through my own efforts to the acclaim of all!

Finally, toward the end of the retreat the experience of love and truth in the heart of God broke through my desire to be so worthy. God's love was made real through the gentle care of my director and other friends who made the retreat with me. The truth came in the almost too good to be true "Good News" that I already am holy (but only as pure gift of God), and some wisdom has been given. What is more, I stand on holy ground and encounter holy people all around me, not perfect, but holy and good by God's design. What freedom that brings! It's all *good*—given in creation, sustained as *good* by the *Good Spirit* of all being.

One of the last nights I had a dream: I was admitted to the hospital amid great concern that something was seriously wrong. An older doctor was sticking me with hypodermic needles, taking blood for all kinds of tests and shaking his head as though I didn't have a ghost of a chance. I resisted physically, even violently, then finally gave in. And wonder of wonders, when all the tests were in, there was nothing seriously wrong with me!—

only a few symptoms of my own making. A dream like that is not too hard to interpret given the context.

I close with a quote from St. Therese Couderc, Cenacle Foundress, that sums up the "grace" of the retreat:

> ... I saw written in letters of gold that word "Goodness," which I kept repeating for a long time with indescribable sweetness; I saw it, I say, written upon all creatures, animate and inanimate, rational or otherwise—all bore this name "Goodness." I even saw it upon the chair which served me for *prie-dieu*. I understood then that all the good creatures have ... and all the services and help we receive from each of them, are a benefit we owe to the goodness of our God, who has communicated to them something of his infinite goodness so that we might find it in everything and everywhere.[5]

Stories of Ferment

Stories of ferment, for the believer, are ultimately stories of Hope. Literature reveals the human propensity for undaunted hope in the midst of persecution, war and tribulation. Dreams are born in the face of such adversity. It takes big hearts and generous hands to begin to shape the dreams into reality. As we rake the ashes of lost loves and broken dreams of adversity, we begin to choose which seeds we will nourish in our hearts, and the harvest follows in kind.

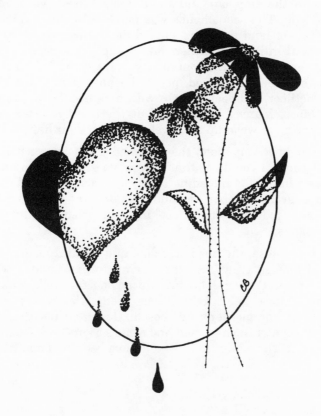

In Search of the Promised Land

For me, the story of José and the community of Nimajuyú began with my very first trip into plantation country with Father John. As the four-wheel drive pickup bounced and grunted, John commented, "There never used to be a road here. This is all new." Grabbing the door handle tighter, I asked, "Are you sure we're on a road now?"

After twenty minutes of steep inclines and sharp switchbacks, we came to the tiny one-and-a-half room school where Mass would be said. The schoolhouse was perched in the middle of a narrow strip of land that was shaped like a hog's back with almost vertical gullies on either side. Simple one room shacks, homes of the people of the community, were sprinkled along the ridge. As soon as we arrived, people began drifting toward the school. The floor had been strewn with pine needles in preparation for Mass. Many folks stopped at the nearby water spigot before entering to wash up or to wet and comb their hair.

I noticed how very poor they seemed in their patched and ragged clothing. I could see that this was a growing community; there was a herd of stampeding little boys racing around underfoot and a great number of young children at their mother's breasts and toddlers shyly peeking out from behind their mothers' skirts.

Then I met José, the head catechist and natural leader of the village. He had a crew cut—rare for an Indian—and a warm, gracious smile. Father John introduced me to José's wife and child; the tiniest baby I had ever seen, who was suckling vigorously at her mother's full bosom. José told me that little Victoria, their eighth child, had had some serious problems when she was born. Normally there would have been no hope for her, but with the help of the doctor in the parish clinic, she pulled through.

After Mass, the men gathered to discuss a pressing difficulty. Though stubbornly against violence as a solution to the economic injustices in Guatemala, they were in a vulnerable position. The guerrillas who periodically operate nearby were soliciting food and support. At the same time, the army was pressuring the whole village to move to assure there would be no aid for the insurgents. Intimidation, unwarranted detention and questioning are some of the tactics used to apply pressure. But the options open for moving seemed expensive, at best, or part of a master plan of "population control," at worst. One man mentioned that a certain village, in similar circumstances, moved where the government suggested and found themselves in a situation little better than a concentration camp. So, it seemed unlikely that they would leave.

Over the next year, I went back to Nimajuyú for various celebrations of the Eucharist. I especially enjoyed the warm welcome and a fun time of doing "magic" tricks for the kids. Most of them had never been out of the village nor seen television so they were easily impressed. The adults inspired me with their hope and determined faith in the midst of tremendous tension.

During those months the community had become very charismatic in its style of prayer, especially with the influence of a "prophetess," who claimed visions and messages from God. This is not uncommon in a culture that is, in general, very open to the spiritual world. Though her influence certainly caused some problems, the general impact on the community was of strengthening and enlivening.

José had come to be a special friend. I grew to respect his integrity and his struggle to be a good leader of a community in transition. One day, however, he disappeared! He had been walking to San Lucas to buy medicine for his dying mother and did not return. Rumors immediately suggested a kidnapping by unknown persons, but questions like "Why?", or "Where might he be?", or "Would he ever be seen alive again?" could not be answered.

Father Greg and Father John immediately went to the regional authorities to give a character witness and to plead on his behalf. The villagers also went—a whole truckload of them—begging for his safe return. The fact that they were well received and that no others had disappeared were signs of hope during those anxious days. There was even a rumor that José had been seen in Nimajuyú itself, being escorted further up the mountain by armed men.

As the days stretched into a week, frustration grew and hope faded. The pain was heightened by the death of José's mother after a long illness. In their grief and fear, the community joined together even more tightly as they stormed heaven with their tearful petitions.

For Father John the waiting was very difficult; besides, other matters needed attention. On the morning of the tenth day after José had disappeared, he took the Bronco and headed for the Capital. Fifteen minutes down the road, through the early morning haze, he saw a figure in the ditch. It moved—a hesitant half wave. Then he recognized José. He was standing! He was alive!

He appeared exhausted from a lack of sleep, weak from hunger and possibly hurt; he walked gingerly and protected himself. He had been dumped in the ditch after a nightmare of accusations, interrogations and beatings. Blindfolded and with his hands tied behind his back he had been hit and kicked. He was convinced that they were about to kill him. But eventually they relented and let him go. Who was ultimately responsible for this was not certain. There was talk of two people having a personal grudge against José, but that was only speculation. He was alive and back home—that was the great news.

As Father John excitedly whipped the Bronco around and roared back to San Lucas, the car unexpectedly backfired. José jumped and stiffened thinking it was a gun shot. The ordeal had taken its toll on his nerves. At the "Casa Padres" (priest's house) he savored a breakfast cooked by Father Greg. The doctor was called to examine José. He confirmed that José's badly bruised chest was the result of beatings.

A tearful reunion followed with family and friends. The driver sent to bring the family down the mountain actually had trouble convincing them that José was going to be fine. The request for clean clothes was interpreted to mean that his body had been found and that they were being called to prepare his body for the wake. Finally convinced, they joyfully jammed into the room next to mine, where José would stay for a few days to recover. The sounds of rejoicing and excited stories drifted through the house as well as the unique odor of people who live around open cooking fires.

I had fun entertaining some of his young sons. Actually, I was entertained by them, watching as they discovered a new world of marvelous—even magical—gadgets they had never seen before. Things like a shelf full of books, a tape recorder, a spinning top or animals made of balloons would almost make their eyes pop out and cause smiles to crease their faces. One of them didn't know what the stool in the bathroom was for and obviously thought the wastebasket was the most logical container to use.

The following week was one of continuous celebration both happy and sad. First was the Mass for José's mother, the customary nine days after her death. A few days later was the Mass of Thanksgiving for the safe return of José. They wanted it as *alegre* (festive) as possible, which meant I had to chant all the appropriate parts of the Mass. I had never done that in English, much less Spanish, but I did my best.

The joyful celebration could not be sustained for very long. A few months later, some of the men were again approached in their fields by guerrillas who demanded food. So, again, they found themselves in an impossible situation with threats of violence from both sides.

Looking in from the outside, it seems best that they should move. But how and where can fifty families move at a moment's notice? And what will be the cost; not just financially, but the emotional cost of the uprooting and all the problems that would come from a husband and wife being separated for long periods of time? (The men would have to return to work their land which is the only means of support for their families.)

This story does not have a nice, clean ending. At the time of this writing, the community of Nimajuyú is asking for help to build a church, a temporary one, until they can find the resources to build a permanent one.

Perhaps the story has no ending because it is the story of many groups all over Central America and, in fact, the story of many peoples of all ages. Is it not, for example, the story of the Israelites looking for their promised land—a saving and safe space to live out their lives in peace?

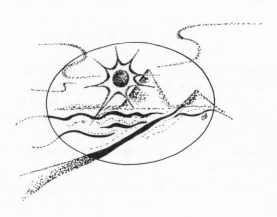

"To have faith is to be sure of the things we hope for, to be certain of things we cannot see." Hebrews 11:1.

Hope Built on Ashes

Someone once asked me, "How are you different after your experience in Guatemala? I tried to share with him what I have learned about Christian hope. I have found myself using the word "hope" much more than I did when I lived in the States. Perhaps that's because the Spanish word for hope, esperanza, *is so rich in meaning; it encompasses waiting, expectation, and hope.*

Before I came here, I would often ask myself and others, "What do you see around you as reasons for hope?" Now my experience tells me that, at its core, hope is not based on reason or "signs." It is, rather, an anchor thrown with confidence into an apparently bottomless sea that must hold or we will drift away. Perhaps it would be more clear if I just share this story.

A messenger burst into the room during our annual diocesan meeting for pastoral planning. He quickly delivered his news to Father Antonio. We didn't need to hear the message to know something terrible had happened. Father Antonio's pale face and sad, glistening eyes communicated enough. He got up quickly and left without a word.

He returned two days later, still visibly shaken, to tell an incredible tale. There had been a calamitous fire. All was lost—except hope.

In his rather progressive parish, a cooperative had been formed in an attempt to provide support for the many widows and unemployed who were scattered throughout the surrounding hills. Taking advantage of a special U.S. law that cuts all import tax on certain products from developing Caribbean countries, they proposed to market woven baskets and *ocote* in North

America. (*Ocote* is the very flammable, sap-filled wood taken from the core of pine trees. It is an excellent fire starter for wood burning stoves and fire places.)

After forming the working groups and gathering the raw materials, they began production. Hundreds of people were involved. Within a few months, they had filled the huge warehouse next to the church with $42,000 worth of these products. It was almost ready to ship. Of course, because of its high value, a full-time guard had to stand watch.

One of the guards was Juan, a young man about 22 years old, who was a longtime, trusted employee of the parish. He, his wife and their two little girls formed one of those model families that seem much too rare.

While Juan was on duty late one evening, he heard some cries for help coming from the nearby house. Hurrying over, he surprised a government service man forcing himself on a young woman he knew. In the confusion of the moment, she escaped to safety and Juan backed away from a dangerous confrontation. But he had evidently seen too much already.

The government agent and some friends returned a few nights later to make sure he wouldn't talk. They disarmed him and began to beat him severely. They warned him never to tell anyone about the rape incident. Suddenly, Juan went limp and stopped breathing.

The men realized that they had gone too far and now they looked for a way to destroy any evidence. Dragging the body inside the warehouse, they threw it on top of the pile of *ocote* and started a fire. Within minutes, the whole place was an inferno. Within hours, there was nothing left but ashes.

Bits of this story quickly came forth from the girl and various other sources. They searched and found what remained of Juan.

Father Antonio celebrated the funeral the next day. Understandably, he and the whole parish were in shock. Not only had they lost a friend to stupid and brutal violence, but it also seemed that with Juan a community dream had gone up in smoke. After all their efforts in selling the project, motivating the people, and actually doing the back-breaking work, the question weighed heavily, "Is it still possible to hope for a better world—a new heaven and a new earth?" (Rev. 21:1). "Is it worth the struggle?"

Father Antonio was hardly out of the sacristy after the funeral Mass when one of his workers approached him and said, "We've been talking among ourselves, Padre, and we know if we don't work quickly, we will lose the market in the United States. We are ready to call the people together tomorrow and start over again."

That is hope built on ashes!

> "We who have found safety with him are greatly encouraged to hold firmly to the hope placed before us. We have this hope as an anchor for our lives. It is safe and sure, and goes through the curtain of the heavenly temple into the inner sanctuary." Hebrews 6:18b-19.

"Forgive them, Father! They don't know what they are doing." Luke 23:24

A Father Forgives

This story was shared with me before I came to Guatemala, before I knew much of its culture and present struggle. I had been contemplating the possibility of being a missionary and I remember wanting to know, personally, a people and culture that could give birth to such a story.

The setting is Santiago Atitlán, a town of 40,000 people, almost all Guatemalan Indians, that has suffered for many years the degradation of poverty and the terror of political violence. Paradoxically, it is famous as a tourist stop because of the beauty of its natural surroundings and its attractive native customs and dress.

The impossible living situation of the majority of its inhabitants has made it a seedbed of political unrest and a target for those charged with preserving the *status quo*. For example, a large extended family of twenty to thirty people might be crowded into the space of a typical North American front yard. Being primarily nickel and dime merchants without land of their own, they have nowhere to expand. Some live lives of quiet desperation. Others push with whatever means are available to survive in the present and secure a future for their children.

Diego and his family were *not* the passive types. Besides his wife, there were three sons in their early twenties and two younger daughters. He taught them how to survive in the marketplace. They were neither cheats nor thieves, but their aggressiveness was well known and won them various envious enemies. They were also believing, church-going Christians who knew the example of Jesus in his forgiving love.

So it happened during the height of the violence that the boys were accused of being guerrillas. Who made the charge or why was not known. Little provocation was needed and there was no investigation to verify the accusations.

First the eldest son, Diego (Jr.) disappeared on his way back from selling in the Capital. They found his tortured body in a ravine along the highway. Then, one evening, armed men surrounded the house of his second son. Carlos was not home but was expected to come by bus in a few hours. Neighbors informed his father that Carlos was in danger. Diego frantically searched for a way to stop the horror that seemed to be unfolding.

He decided to hire a car to take him to San Lucas where the bus would pass. He hoped to board the bus and warn Carlos to turn back and never come home again. But he was not found on that bus! Not knowing what else to do, Diego returned to Santiago heavy with grief and a profound sense of powerlessness.

The next day, a companion of Carlos told Diego what had happened. He and Carlos had done well selling their avocados and were returning home on an earlier bus. Between San Lucas and Santiago they were forced by unknown persons to get off and show their identification papers. Carlos and another man were detained while the rest were allowed to continue.

Diego's heart sank even lower as he realized there was little to do now except wait and look for more bodies. This time none were found. Nothing more was heard of the two that were taken. The silence was deafening. The fears ran wild. When would it all end?

A reporter came through months later trying to pursue the story. In an interview he asked Diego, "After all that has happened to your family—one son brutally murdered, another missing and presumed dead and not knowing at what moment another of your family or you yourself might be taken and killed, are you revengeful and bitter toward those who have done this to you?" Slowly and sadly Diego responded, "No. . . If I would be full of bitterness I have allowed them to kill me as well."

"If it were an enemy making fun of me I could endure it; if it were an opponent boasting over me I could hide myself from him. But it is you, my companion, my colleague and close friend." Psalm 55:12-13.

Mario, the Fisherman

We had fish today for dinner, and it isn't even a Friday in Lent. It was good—black bass, fresh from the lake. As we squeezed on the lemon, Father John reminded me of a fisherman's story. Like so many stories that are lived out in this culture, it seems to have an echo in the pages of Scripture. Every time I read Psalm 55, I think of Mario.

Mario comes from Cerro de Oro (Hill of Gold). The "hill" is really a small volcano nestled close to the shore of Lake Atitlán overlooking Mario's house. He lives there with his wife and three young children.

Every morning at five o'clock during fishing season, Mario carefully places his nylon gill net into his canoe and heads out alone to test his skill. It is a challenge since the lake has been taken over by the carnivorous bass that have all but eliminated the other species. The best spots are now over-fished as many fishermen try to make a little extra money and, at the same time, add some badly needed protein to their diet.

Mario used to go out fishing now and then with his friend, Lucas, but not anymore. That was before the trouble between them began. They had even gone together to look for a new canoe for Lucas. Mario used his influence to get a good price. In the unwritten law of the land, Lucas owed Mario a favor. He proved later not to be a man of honest accounts.

One evening, while Mario and his family were attending a church service, someone broke into his supply shack and stole his new fish net. Mario was angry and even frightened. He and his wife had exhausted their meager savings and spent two months tying the nylon line into a two inch grid. How could they start over again? What would they live on? He regretted not marking it clearly with his name, but after spending so much time making it, he could recognize it easily. He hoped he might recover it somehow.

A few weeks later, he heard Lucas was fishing with a new net and went to check out where he had gotten it. Though he could not prove it, Mario was shocked to discover that it was really the missing net. Confronted with the truth, Lucas denied any knowledge of the robbery. He claimed he had bought the net in San Lucas with money that he had been saving for years.

Mario felt so betrayed and disheartened that he walked away and never spoke to Lucas again. Without proof of some kind, he would get nowhere in a civil complaint. Meanwhile, his family needed to eat something besides corn tortillas.

Not long afterwards, Father John went to Cerro de Oro. Needing to tell his story, Mario spoke to him after Mass. Almost paraphrasing Psalm 55, he shared the hurt caused by the betrayal of his friend. "I could understand if he were an enemy, but we were partners. I even went with him to buy a canoe so he might get a better deal from a man I knew." Father John also heard the desperate need for money to buy the line and sinkers to make another net. Mario could not promise to repay him, but he would try.

Since then, every few months, Mario comes in with a gift of gratitude. He also visits a little with Father John, recounting how things are going.

That is why we had fish today. And not only is it a delicious meal, but it is also a reminder of our mission here that involves a commitment to work for a just society, one that would diminish the chances that this story would happen again.

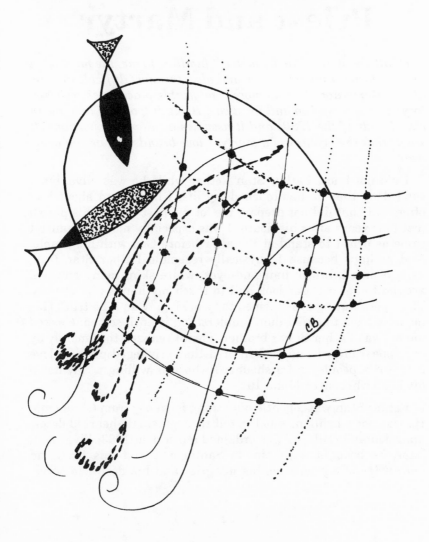

"The greatest love a person can have for his friends is to give his life for them." John 15:13

Father Stan Rother: Priest and Martyr

Of all the stories this is the most familiar to me, the most often retold whenever visitors come, and also, the most difficult to write down. Martyrdom has its more comfortable place in church history; that is, long ago and far away. Bring it too close to home in this decade of the 1980s and it assumes awesome proportions. It seems that the mystery of a martyr's love brands you as you draw near.

I did not know Father Stan Rother while he was alive, but I can't deny that he has touched my life. I had heard about him often, but that did not prepare me for my first visit to his parish just four years after his death. I was especially moved because I came as priest to stand at the altar before God with his people. And perhaps because I physically resemble Father Stan (tall, thin, bearded, brown hair and eyes, white skin) many crowded around to get a closer look and to touch my hands and clothes. Their penetrating eyes seemed to be asking, "Can it be true? Has he come back to us?" I didn't understand it until someone asked me if I was Father Stan's brother. Then I realized that merely by my appearance, I had encountered that privileged place of love between a people and a shepherd who was willing to lay down his life for his sheep (John 10).

Father Stan was a gentle but strong farm boy from Oklahoma. He was not a brilliant scholar, but through single-hearted determination and faith, he was ordained a priest in 1963. Five years later, he brought with him to Santiago Atitlan his firsthand knowledge of agriculture, his integrity and his desire to serve.

Over the next thirteen years he slowly became one with the struggles, hopes and joys of the native people. He endeared himself to them as he learned their language, worked along side them with his hands, and became known as *buena gente*—a compassionate man whose word is true.

As his beloved people began to suffer from the political violence in the late '70s and especially 1980-81, it is no wonder that he reacted strongly and spoke out boldly denouncing the crimes against his people. Accustomed to "telling it as it is," he soon found himself siding with his native friends and catechists as they lived in an atmosphere full of constant fear and grief. Over those years in Santiago, literally hundreds were tortured and killed and many more fled seeking safety. Some people were sleeping in the church to avoid the death squads.

In January of 1981, Father Stan and his associate had to flee because their lives were definitely in danger. Stan went to the States and continued to decry the atrocities that were happening in Guatemala. His message was reported to the United States State Department and possibly relayed back to Guatemala. This may have sealed his fate in the end.

During his time away, Father Stan grew more and more restless. He missed his people and did not want to think he was like a hireling who ran away at the first sign of danger. They were being "snatched and scattered." Now was their greatest need for a good shepherd.

After five months, without any guarantees for his safety, he returned to his parish. Six priests had already been killed in the country. Over 100,000 Guatemalans were murdered or disappeared, mostly poor Indians caught in a struggle beyond their control.

At first, things seemed to be tense but calmer. There were no new disappearances. The parish celebrated their big *fiesta* as usual on July 25. Then, on the night of July 28, unknown armed men broke into the rectory. Surprising a parish worker inside, they demanded that he show them where Father Stan was sleeping. The young worker tried to save Stan by saying that he was not home that night. The intruders then threatened to kill the young man right there if he did not immediately do as they asked. Terrified, he pointed out Stan's door, then he was locked in a separate room.

There were sounds of an intense struggle. Father Stan would not let them take him out of the house. Finally two shots were heard, then nothing but silence.

The next morning, he was found by the sisters who lived in the same parish complex. They raced to San Lucas to inform the priests there. Father Greg went to stay with the body while Father John made it in record time to the nearest phone to call Stan's parents and the American embassy.

Meanwhile, the people in Santiago were so outraged that they were ready to take up their machetes against those they believed were responsible. One of the sisters probably averted a great massacre by keeping the people in the church singing hymns of resurrection for Father Stan.

Another crisis emerged over where he was to be buried. His parents had requested that his body be flown back to Oklahoma. However, the people knew that Stan had wanted to be buried in Guatemala. They were determined to honor his request and bury their beloved pastor with their own relatives. Finally, a few of the leaders agreed to go with Father John to talk to Stan's mother and father once more. His parents remained resolute. Father John turned from the phone and said, "Father Stan's parents say that you have had their son for thirteen years. Now that he is dead they want him home with them." Finally, the men agreed to try to convince the people to release the body. One of them said, "We understand the terrible pain of not being able to have a son's body buried with your other loved ones. Many of us know that same pain. It is right that he be buried with his family."

In the prescribed autopsy after such a death, the heart and blood were taken and placed in a jar apart from the body. That crystal jar was placed on the altar for the Mass of Resurrection where it was visible to all. Afterward, the people's consolation was to be able to bury this part of Father Stan in back of the altar in Church. Since blood is believed to be the source of life and the heart, the seat of love, they felt they had been true to Stan's request as well.

It has been noted throughout history that the faith flourishes in the face of persecution. Like rain in the desert, the blood of martyrs seems to give birth to flowers of promise—hope for tomorrow.

In those initial hours and days after Father Stan's murder, those close to him struggled with the seeming absurdity of martyrdom. As the rage and grief subsided, the fruits of his sacrifice slowly became more evident. His blood, poured out in this land of conflict, has become a source and symbol of life. It is a river of hope on whose banks the seeds of Christians sprout and grow tall.

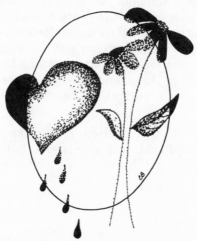

"Instead of eating, I mourn and I can never stop groaning." Job 3:24

A Modern-Day Job

There are some sad stories—very sad—almost too much to bear. This is the story of a modern-day Job.

Actually, his name is Pedro. He was strong, good-looking and a hard worker. He and his wife, Fidelia, were joined about eighteen years ago. They started their life together with great hope and much love—a love that soon found concrete expression in babies that came along about every other year. They were poor and could hardly feed the children, but they struggled on.

Soon the hard life began to take its toll. Of the seven children, first little Walter died. He made it to his first birthday but no further. Then another little boy, Jeronimo, didn't even make it through his first day. Young children die so frequently here that these deaths were barely noted by friends and neighbors.

A few years later, Father Greg went down to a village and came back shaking his head and pondering. He had been with the community of Pampojilá as it buried one of its young mothers. No one was sure of the exact reason why Fidelia had died, but there seemed to be an uncomfortable consensus that hope had just slipped away from her and she simply gave up the struggle. Not that she took any active means to end her life as had three others from that same community that year (usually by drinking poison), but without the desire to live, Fidelia slowly withered away.

That left Pedro with five children. They picked up and tried to carry on. The oldest, Paula, was only twelve, but she became the primary homemaker and "mother" while Pedro tried to make enough to live on.

About eight months later I was trying to get away from the parish center to celebrate a Mass down in the plantations when two men boldly stopped my car. One was half drunk, the other silent and sober. Slowly, with a voice filled with grief and self-pity, Pedro begged for the money to build a rough wooden coffin for his little girl turned "mother." Paula had been quite normal— up and around, doing her daily chores—then, as best as I could understand through the alcohol and the tears, she died a few hours later from a combination of diarrhea and vomiting. The money was quickly arranged. As I drove back toward San Lucas after Mass, I saw the coffin being carried down the road. Pedro was half stumbling, half running along behind; his world totally out of control inside and out.

I felt relieved, remembering that I was already booked for the next day. Again Father Greg returned from the funeral visibly shaken. He had asked what had happened to the girl, and one of the neighbors revealed that during the preparation of the body for burial, it became clear that the cause of death was parasitic worms!

I shuddered as I imagined Pedro seeing them and realizing what had happened. No wonder that he had continued to drink through the day of the funeral. No one could say whether he would be able to begin again.

It seems he did bounce back but not for long. Tragedy struck once more. This time tuberculosis was the villain and his daughter, Margarita, the victim. After a year of being practically bedridden, she, like her mother, withered to nothing but skin and bones, then died.

It was after her funeral that the pieces of this story were connected for me, and I wondered about the end of the story for this modern-day Job. I wanted to believe in full restoration but that seemed absurd—especially as I saw Pedro's body absorbing all that pain and sorrow. His legs would no longer hold him. As he grieved, the community often gathered around his bed to pray with him. They offered tortillas for the remaining children. They helped pay his medical bills from the last ordeal.

Slowly, he got back on his feet. There has been no dramatic restoration, but a few weeks ago he came asking for new tin roofing for his little cornstalk house. And I bought a basket from him that he had woven that day. Although he still cannot do heavy labor, he has turned to commercial buying and selling to make a dollar or so a day. When I stop to think about it, after all that has happened, to end this story with even this glimmer of hope is to revisit in some small way the last chapter of the Book of Job.

"The Lord blessed the last part of Job's life even more than the first . . . Job lived a hundred and forty years after this, long enough to see his grandchildren and great-grandchildren. And then he died at a very great age." Job 42:12a; 16-17

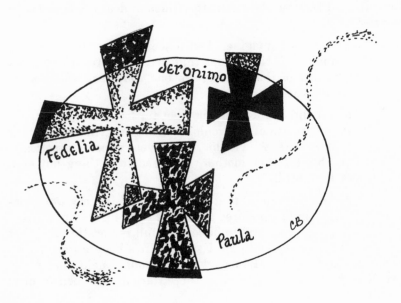

The Movement

*I returned to San Lucas by the hot coast road, though I knew
there might be trouble because the farm laborer's march for land
was moving toward the Capital. I could have avoided it completely by taking a detour, but I was curious about the progress and
organization. I was supportive of their cause.*

The demonstration had been splashed in the newspaper head-
lines for several days. To make their cry for land heard, nineteen
thousand farm laborers were marching in unison a hundred
miles to the Capital. Led by the charismatic and courageous
Father Andrés Girón, they headed for the National Palace to
force an audience with the president.

When I met them on the road, there was no problem; everyone
walked in perfect order, six to eight abreast, filling exactly half
the road. Most wore white shirts, carried a hoe or machete, and a
shoulder bag with their lunch. Some were barefoot but moved
with the rest across the steaming pavement.

I pulled over to absorb the scene and to marvel at the impres-
sion they left. Questions popped into my mind as they filed by for
ten minutes. What is the urgent need that unites them? Why are
they marching now? Is there any hope that their cry will be
heard? Will they live to tell their children about this historic
march?

The first question is easy to answer in a country where about
eighty-five percent of the land is owned by ten percent of the
people; they are united in a movement to obtain land, not only
because that presumes a more equitable sharing of the earth's
resources, but also they want to live. Without land, many of
them and their children will die from malnutrition and related
illnesses. Land is a basic economic and political issue in all of

Latin America; without land there are no tortillas; without tortillas there is no life.

Secondly, they were marching at that specific time to call attention to the land issue in general, and more specifically, to put pressure on the banks to change a policy which requires that large tracks of repossessed land be purchased by a single buyer. Such a policy makes it very difficult for poor farmers to find small, affordable pieces of available land.

Yes, they were met and heard. Nineteen thousand people on a protest march, representing literally millions more and forcing a media scene on the most sensitive political topic, cannot be ignored by a still unstable democracy. The president and many other top officials even offered to come out into the country to meet them in an attempt to defuse the situation, but Padre Giron said he wanted to take the issue to the government center. He wanted his message to be heard.

They were not heard in the sense that banking policy has been changed to allow individuals to get loans for small plots. However, the need for agrarian reform was made clear and they were allowed to collectively buy one farm that would support four hundred and fifty families on a profit sharing basis.

Whether they will live to tell their children or grandchildren about the movement, who can say. At this point, four of the marchers have disappeared, but there is hope that these will reappear, and no others will be terrorized. Neither is too likely, considering how much is at stake. And what is at stake is that portion of material goods that is extra for the wealthy few who, for fear of losing everything, fight with every means possible, including violence, to preserve their social and financial position.

I went to visit Padre Girón about a year and a half after they had taken over the farm. I wanted to ask him about the movement and about some details of the march. I found a man, tired from the burden and stress of his work, but persistent in speaking clearly the truth about the reality of the land situation and what must happen for future progress of Guatemala.

I enjoyed some of his stories about the march: how food was donated and prepared by thousands along the route, how others tried to sabotage the mission by giving out hundreds of bottles of free liquor (all the bottles were turned over to him still full), and how the officials' preoccupation with toilet facilities for nineteen thousand people in downtown Guatemala City was solved by merely telling the folks to use the fields before they entered the city. They didn't even touch the portable toilets that were anxiously brought in.

He spoke with pride about how the collective farm was turning a profit. After paying a salary and benefits far above normal for farm laborers, they were able to pay off their production loan and, in addition, give each family four hundred dollars. (Four hundred dollars represents eight months' wages for the average farm worker.) He mentioned how people entering the movement must agree to give five percent of the profits toward the purchase of more land for other families. This, with the help of money from European communities, will buy land for fifteen hundred more families. And with particular animation, he shared that he had just received a license to export agricultural products.

Given the reality, these are amazing accomplishments in a short amount of time. Realizing the danger that he is choosing to live with every day, I was moved to pray for his safety and for wisdom in his decisions.

Driving back to San Lucas, I thought about the life and death struggle taking place over the land. It called to mind an era in North America when the land absorbed the blood of people fighting for the opportunity that the land offers. Perhaps Chief Seattle's words speak of a truth that all peoples will eventually come to know. In this there is hope.

"We are part of the earth and it is part of us . . . The earth is our mother. This we know. The earth does not belong to us, we belong to the earth. All things are connected like the blood which unites one family. Our God is the same God. You may think now that you own God as you wish to own our land, but you cannot. God is the God of all peoples and God's compassion is equal . . . the earth is precious to God." (Chief Seattle's Speech, 1834)[6]

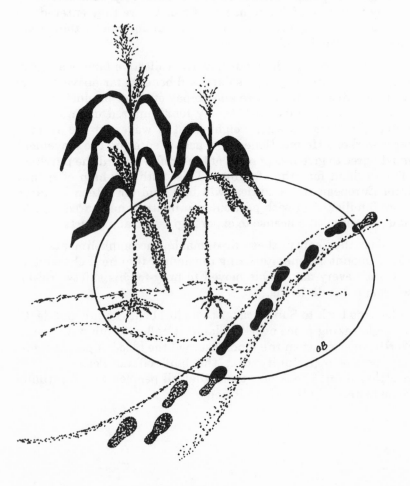

Water That Gives Life

Second only to the struggle for land, the issue that most preoccupies Guatemala is water. Most of the rural area is lush and green during the rainy season, but the dry season is six months long and there are only ten lakes of mentionable size in the whole country. Thus, in order to flourish, the communities must do a delicate balancing act between the land that is available and the sources of water. What follows is the impressive story of one village's successful effort to bring water to their houses on their own land.

I was invited to celebrate Mass at San Gabriel soon after I arrived at the mission. Not yet understanding that they were rejoicing in a dream come true, I was overwhelmed to see the whole community gathering around a single water faucet in the small school courtyard. There were flowers and decorative leaves around the flowing spigot and pine needles covering the ground. Being six-feet-four inches tall among a people that average four-feet-eleven, I bumped my head—to the enjoyment of all—on the temporary roof that they had erected for the occasion. Evidently they intended to give thanks and celebrate for a significant length of time. And they did.

Four years later, they got up the courage to ask me to offer a Mass of Blessing and Thanksgiving at the source of their life-giving water. Having come to appreciate the importance of water, I quickly said, "Yes, of course!", but I didn't know what it would require. I arranged to come at nine the next Saturday morning to meet whomever would take me to the spring where the people would be waiting. I couldn't imagine it would be far if the whole village was going to be there.

Luckily, I chose the four-wheel drive pickup. During that trip I finally came to understand this community's water rituals and the particular pride they have in their accomplishment.

First, we drove in a half circle for one-half hour, deep into the most rugged mountains in the area. At times the twisting road was passable only in first gear, so steep were the inclines. The rocky canyons and gorgeous tree-covered slopes kept trying to pull my eyes from the narrow road. Finally we could drive no more.

Now it was time to put on the hiking boots. Down into the valley we trotted. I was grateful for the man who offered to carry the Mass kit. I apologized for bringing the big one, but it didn't seem to be a burden to him. As the path wound down, music from an accordion and, of all things, an electric bass drifted up filling the valley. When we drew closer we could hear the people singing and someone talking over a loudspeaker.

I groaned as the trail headed up the other side. However, I knew there was hope that I would make it. The vegetation, green from sinking its roots in the overflow from the spring, told me we only had a few hundred yards to go.

We followed the four-inch pipe to the most extraordinary stage and amphitheatre I have ever seen. I immediately regretted forgetting my camera. The tubing from three different water projects led up to a cement holding tank dug into the side of the hill. On top of the cement slab were placed the altar and other "essential" things: flowers in vases, candles, lots of incense and a chair for the Padre!

More than a hundred people were seated on the forest hillside—men, women, and children. I even counted ten nursing babies, including a little five-pounder I had just baptized a week earlier. The canopy of trees shaded us from the bright sun while the music from the combo and the throbbing of the ram-pump drew us to the source of all life-giving water.

The responsorial psalm of the day spoke to the heart of the matter.

"O God, you are my God, and I long for you.
My whole being desires you.

Like a dry, worn-out, and waterless land,
my soul is thirsty for you.

Let me see you in the sanctuary;
let me see how mighty and glorious you are.

Your constant love is better than life itself,
and so I will praise you.

I will give thanks as long as I live;
I will raise my hands to you in prayer.

My soul will feast and be satisfied,
and I will sing glad songs of praise to you."
                                        —Psalm 63:1-5

It was for me one of those choice moments that makes priest-hood so precious to me. There were no walls to the church in which we prayed, but never have I felt more one with the people of God as the powerful sign of our common baptism gushed from under my feet and from under the legs of the altar of sacrifice.

After Mass I listened to Martin, the head of the water project, tell how it came to be. Ten years earlier, San Gabriel and three other communities had bought the rights to the spring. Then came the long process of receiving permission to cross the land of every owner between the source and final destination eight miles away. The materials were donated by various developmental agencies, but the labor was done with picks, axes and shovels by the members of the village. It took them one full year to dig a trench and bury that pipe in the mountainous terrain.

Martin pointed out the barely visible switchbacks of the trail that followed the pipe out of a distant canyon and on toward their village. I shook my head as I gazed in awe across the huge valley at least ten times deeper and wider than the one we had just walked down. It was clear why we couldn't come to the spring by the direct route.

He told me that ten years ago, when they started the project, he had told the committee that it would be proper to get a priest to come and bless the spring, but it was too dangerous because of the political violence in the area.

For Martin who knows the Source of All Living Water, the gathering around the water hole was another dream come true. For the moment, his thirst was satisfied.

Freedom Train

It was time for my annual trip home to visit and raise funds. I decided to travel by land through Mexico to experience more of the vast expanse of land and diverse Latin culture that separated Guatemala from the United States.

The adventure began with a 24-hour bus ride to Mexico City. A storm had stirred up the atmosphere, causing a steady rain throughout that first day and night. I arrived in Mexico City with cramped legs and exhausted from a lack of sleep and the tension of the storm. I was ready for what I thought would be a more leisurely and comfortable train ride to the U.S. border.

I had been advised to buy a ticket for a private compartment that included a bed long enough for my lanky frame. Unfortunately the compartments were all filled. The best I could get (a step down from the individual compartments) was an assigned seat on the "Special 1st Class" car. The whole experience of riding a Mexican train was new to me and I didn't know what to expect.

Arriving early for boarding I began to notice some curious things. Separate entrances led to the loading dock—one for the sleeping compartments and 1st Class, the other for 2nd and 3rd Class. I had come early and found few at my gate, but the long line for the lower class already stretched from the loading platform to the front door of the depot. Each minute the line grew longer with breathless people rushing up and anxiously crowding close to those in front of them. I didn't know whether they didn't want anyone to butt in line or were afraid that there would not be room on the train. My ticket had only cost me the equivalent of about forty-five dollars for the thirty-eight hour trip, but the uncommon and uncomfortable realization settled in that I was one of the few "rich" who could afford an assigned seat.

As the gates opened I observed the stampede on my right as the lower class passengers scrambled for a seat. They all seemed to get on quite quickly so I assumed that there was plenty of room. I returned to my personal concern about the possibility of securing a bed for the next night if one might be vacated along the way. I even slipped the conductor a little "reminder" bill to further my chances. My conscience didn't bother me as I spent the second restless night in a row twisting and turning like a rubber pretzel.

The beautiful sunrise that morning over the interesting desert landscape lifted my spirits. A half-hour stop for food sold by the local vendors on the dock also helped clear the aches remaining from the long night. I even felt good enough to do some bargain shopping—something I don't do unless I feel great. And to top it off, the conductor came by to offer me a bed for the following night.

Soon we were rolling again through what seemed like an endless wasteland sprinkled with dead or dying little railroad villages. Some looked like the bombed out remains of a set from an old black and white western movie. My mood began to change again as I observed this rural poverty and the sad eyes that followed the slow train as it wound its way north. I noticed that now with each stop more and more of the simply dressed folk were climbing aboard while very few were getting off. "Where would they be going," I wondered.

Suddenly, it dawned on me. Many of these were the "illegal aliens" starting the journey toward their dream of the promised land in the north (*El Norte*). Fueled by thoughts about material blessings that money can buy, they dream of liberation from the brutal circle of poverty they have known. With desperate hope, they scramble for a place on the "freedom train," unaware of the struggle ahead, unaware that, for many, this illusion will end only in sweat and tears and discrimination.

Finally, at the last major stop, a huge crowd waited to climb aboard the already bulging cars. This I had to see, but stepping down to the platform, I could only watch for a short time before it became too much for me. It was like the train scene from the movie *Gandhi*. While the premier classes watched curiously, the crowd charged the other cars. Some jammed themselves in without apology, some climbed in the windows or passed little babies through to relatives already inside, and others stood by passively, losing hope.

I turned away, walked over to a sandwich stand and ordered two big hogies. The gal took her time making them and, evidently, I got totally absorbed in what she was doing. I was only twenty feet from the train with my back to the tracks. When I turned around, the 1st Class cars were nowhere in sight. I panicked! My compartment, my secure space, my luggage . . . everything was gone. I ran up to the other cars where there were still hundreds waiting to get on. I ran back to the sandwich lady but before I could ask what happened, her husband calmly said, "Don't worry. They just uncoupled your car and pulled it around the corner to pick up some more 2nd Class cars so everyone can get on."

My heart was still pumping fast as I settled into my seat. A prayer of praise and thanks rose up in me as insight broke through. This train is like life's journey, seeking final liberation. Anxiety runs high as the poor scramble for what appears like limited space while we, the rich (I, now, undeniably among them) arrange our reserved seats, falsely complacent because of what our money, position or insurance seems to secure for us.

In the end, we are all surprised that there is room for everyone on the freedom train.

Stories of Frivolity

Life is either frivolous enough, at times, to be wantonly wasted on what gives us joy or it is not worth living. It is the activities and people with whom we choose to waste time that makes life precious and *love* possible. These stories are told from the amateur's point of view . . . that is, someone who, in the literal sense of the word, engages in art, eating, playing, laughing or some other activity merely for "the love of it." Only the amateur is capable of genuine gratitude.

Reflections of an Ardent Kite Flier

Kites are wonderfully fascinating. At least they have always fascinated me. I remember watching my brothers putting one up almost a mile, then tying it to the orchard fence overnight, and when I woke up there it was dancing in the morning sun. Later, when I was about 18, a few of us Schotzko "big kids" had a contest to see who could design and fly the best kite. One turned out artistically great but didn't fly. Mine flew but looked dumpy. But my brother's—Wow! he must have been inspired because it was simply exciting to fly. It sailed almost straight over head, pulling so hard that the string would begin to hurt our fingers. Though I lost the contest, somehow I inherited my brother's kite and kept it in the corner of my college dormitory room for a couple of years. Every once in awhile, usually with spring fever in the air, I would yield to the urge to see it dance again.

Thank God kite flying is not a lost art in Guatemala. A few weeks before the feasts of All Saints and All Souls I was delighted to notice that little boys began to appear in the streets desperately trying to coax their small, hexagonal kites past the ever present kite-eating electrical wires. (As I look out my window I can count the remnants of twenty-six air disasters tangled in the lines.)

I knew that the feast of All Saints was a special day in Latin America. People go to the cemetery to remember their deceased relatives with flowers, food and prayers. But why did they fly kites? An inquiry here and there revealed that kites, flying freely in the breeze, are symbols of the spirits of the just, happily dancing in the presence of God. What a wonderful expression of faith and hope!

64

Then I heard about a small town, not far from where I was studying Spanish, that is famous for its giant kites. Of course, I had to go and check it out. I found the village streets jammed with thousands of visitors as well as locals flowing in a stream toward the cemetery. Among the throngs floated the huge, round kites carefully carried overhead by excited "pit crews." They were from nine to twenty feet in diameter and true works of art. The supporting structure was usually of cane poles, but the faces were delicate and detailed designs of tissue paper—incredibly beautiful in the afternoon sun. I could not wait to see if they would really fly.

The cemetery was already crowded. People were everywhere— around and on top of the bigger mausoleums or gathered around the heaped-up and decorated dirt graves of their relatives. However, it is obvious that the real show everyone was waiting for was the flight of the giant kites. They were propped up in a row along the downwind side of the cemetery, like the wheels of huge circus wagons waiting for the parade to start.

The wind was gentle, too gentle for the biggest ones, but when it picked up now and then, the teams would spring into action to try to launch their masterpieces. There were kite holders, rope tenders, and finally, the one or two that actually worked the kite back and forth trying to nurse it up into the steadier breeze. They would all scramble back and forth through the sloping cemetery, tripping over graves, getting tangled up in the ropes and daring the spectators to stand in the way. Eventually a dozen or so of the "biggies" were soaring gracefully.

What a sight! At first I tried to capture it all through the eye of my camera, but having spent the film, I just opened my own eyes and entered into the whole scene. I even helped catch one that came down on my head. There was something vital about the whole gathering—and in the cemetery no less! I doubt that cemeteries will ever again hold for me the sinister or eerie images of horror shows. Now when I think of cemeteries, I remember that afternoon of All Saints' Day and smile.

It's not hard to imagine how a day like that affected the little boy inside me. I came away with the seed of a dream. Sometimes I would sit and imagine the size, colors and design of "my kite." Sometimes I would remember the cane and how the ropes were attached to it. Once in a while the dream would break out in conversation and I would run it by one of the workers. I would let them have a quick peek at the dream, then take a reading from their reaction. And the seed grew. Perhaps by next All Saints' Day it would be possible—but I couldn't do it alone.

Finally, I put the question to an energetic lad with a sparkling smile. "Chepe, what do you think of building a giant kite for All Saints' Day this year? Would you like to help me make it and fly it?" The response was, "Sure, we can do it."

So began the process of gathering materials and talking to "experienced" kite flyers who were all willing to offer advice, though often contradictory. Chepe brought the cane from the mountains. Someone else helped me find the right kind of paper, glue and string. Another showed me how to rig it so it would fly like a "tamed" kite should fly. But the colorful design on the front, though perhaps the least important, was mine. I enjoyed putting the finishing artistic touches on it.

All Saints' Day came rushing upon us and all seemed ready. But on that day, as rarely happens (because it is supposed to be the dry season) there was lots of rain and only a tiny breeze. Darn! It was hard to wait, but in a couple of days the weather cleared and the wind picked up to signal an attempt at a maiden flight. Chepe didn't show up at the appointed time. God knows why. The only help was an excited four-year-old who was delighted just to carry my big pair of athletic socks that would likely be used for a tail. That was about all he could handle. We walked toward the lakeshore with a string of little kids trailing along behind.

As I carried the kite over my head my arms grew tired and I thought, "I can't fly this thing alone. I sure hope someone is interested in helping me." I asked two young men if they would be willing to hold it while I took the cord and ran. They agreed but with little enthusiasm. The whole effort was a colossal failure. The kite made a tight loop before crashing to the ground. However, it attracted the attention of many on the beach who rallied to the cause. A few soldiers on maneuvers even stopped to joke and offer advice. "You need more tail," one said. I asked him for his extra socks, but he laughed and claimed he didn't have any.

Then, running up from the beach, came a young man in his swimming suit, an artist by profession. He was so eager that he was still dripping with the soap he had forgotten to rinse off in his hurry to get in on the action.

He took over. First, he supervised the addition of a long tail. Next, he grabbed the string while I held the kite until it took off. On the second try, after adding still more rags and socks, he worked it back and forth with the skill that only experience can give. He got it out over the lake where the steady breeze caught it and lifted it high overhead. Like the little kid who is able to hold the string only after daddy gets the kite up, I was able to hang on for awhile. And, of course, I needed more advice about what to do when the wind got too strong. The kite started taking huge, swooping dives toward the water. I was delighted! I, in turn, shared the string and my joy with little four-year-old Greggie and the other kids that crowded around in wonder and awe.

We decided that next year we would go to the cemetery and add our kite to the memorial dance in the sky and join the party amid the tombstones.

"Padre Choi"

I've had a nickname since my first visit to San Lucas. In the local native dialect it means "Father Mouse." The young Indian cooks delight in calling it out as I walk by the kitchen. I really don't mind. I deserve it, I suppose, after teasing them so much.

When I came to Guatemala, knowing that, here, children come by the dozen and not one at a time, I brought along my bag of clown tricks. One of their favorites was a little gray mouse that would come "alive" in my hands. I call him Freddy.

Well, Freddy jumped out of my pocket one of those first evenings as we sat jabbering around the supper table and the girls were clearing the dishes. Rats and mice are common in homes here but *not* as pets. So Freddy made quite a splash on his debut. Even the North American staff thought he was real for a few days and I never told the girls otherwise.

That week I had my first experience with amoebic dysentery. That, combined with nausea, made sleep difficult. One night, as I lay awake thinking about the importance of good plumbing, I heard a real mouse rustling around in the wastebasket. My mind raced ahead and saw the opportunity for a little more fun. I quietly got up and dropped the basketball in the wastebasket trapping the *choi* in the space below.

The amoeba medicine had settled my system by early morning, and I was ready to take a two-day sightseeing trip to the highlands. Since my Spanish was still practically nil, Father

Greg helped me write a note for the unsuspecting cooks. It read, "Here is Freddy. I can't take him with me, so please watch over my little friend and feed him until I get back. Thanks, Padre Felipe." Then I set the basket with the mouse and ball in the middle of the kitchen floor and left.

I could not have anticipated the drama that I created in my absence. The girls were afraid to take the basketball out, so they waited a full day. A sense of obligation finally overcame their fear, and one cautiously lifted the ball and found a pathetic little creature all but dead. Lack of oxygen and the moisture in the basket from cleaning it after I had gotten sick did him in.

When there were no more signs of life, not knowing what to do, practically in tears, they went to Father Greg to ask his advice. They thought they had killed my little Freddy by not taking care of him sooner. Not knowing me well enough as yet, they asked him the urgent question, "Will he be angry with us? What should we do?" Father Greg continued to play along. He replied, "I don't know. Do whatever you think is best."

Walking up to the rectory upon my return, I could see I was awaited with anxious anticipation. Little black heads popped out of the doorway, then disappeared again. When I entered the house they gathered around and silently led me back to my room. I didn't know what had happened and tried to read their faces. Anxiety was evident in their serious expressions but also a mischievous twinkle shone in their eyes.

They opened the door and gestured toward a table in the corner. I roared with laughter and they quickly joined in. On top of the white table cloth were two burning candles and a bouquet of flowers. There was also a beautifully woven wreath of fresh flowers and greens. In the middle of the wreath was a card that said, "Freddy, rest in peace," and in front of that a tiny black casket about the size of a mouse.

Ever since, I have been "Padre Choi." I was even given a white rat for Christmas one year. I named him Freddy II. I gave him away. It's not that I don't like a noisy, munching rat in my bedroom; it's just that a little ten-year-old friend, Olga, had one just like it. It got out of its box and the neighbor's cat ate it. She was sad so I gave her my Freddy II. He's happier for all the loving attention that she gives him.

A Long Lost Brother

Father Ken Wendinger served at San Lucas for only two years but he is remembered with affection. The mention of his name can always spread a smile across even the most serious faces. Ken enjoyed a good joke and left behind a trail of good stories.

Father Ken is famous, among other things, for his "love" of dogs. I speak with tongue in cheek here because once when he returned to Guatemala a sign mysteriously appeared along the road, "Look out, DOGS! Here comes Padre Ken." You see, his car had a tendency to head directly for the mangy, half dead dogs that wander the streets of this country. But I am digressing a bit because this story is not about dogs but about Ken and the donkeys.

In this mountainous region, men do the work of mules, or so it seemed to Father Greg. He thought that carrying one hundred pounds of corn, fertilizer, wood or coffee up and down the valleys and hills, sometimes for miles, must have a diminishing effect on the human spirit. Are we or are we not more than animals? So an all points bulletin was put out to look for some mules. No luck! But they did turn up a pair of donkeys way out on the east coast. They decided that donkeys would be better anyway because they reproduce themselves whereas mules do not. Soon everyone could have one to do his heavy hauling.

It was a great idea whose time had not yet come. The problem with donkeys is they don't like to do mule's work any more than men do. It was soon discovered that the reputation of donkeys as stubborn beasts is well founded. Thus began long hours of training designed to convince the critters that their destiny was to patiently and obediently carry men's burdens. The lot fell to Father Ken to give the lessons. The sessions were grueling for man and beast. In spite of gentle and otherwise very insistent persuasion, the *burros* remained quite unmanageable.

Father John even tried to lend a hand one day, thinking that if you mount the animal with a good stout "persuader" in hand the beast would submissively climb the hill. He was partially correct. That little charcoal donkey hustled right up, but once there, looked for a large tree with a low hanging branch. Soon Father John was picking himself up from the ground and running after the donkey with stick in hand, all to the delight of the curious onlookers.

Once, Father Ken was taking a break as professor in the donkey school and he heard Father Greg giving a talk to the Catholic Action group in the church. That was all he needed. He grabbed one of the halters and led the donkey up the steps, down the center aisle and, reaching the front, genuflected solemnly. Turning around slowly he said, "I would like to introduce to you Father Greg's long lost brother!" Of course, the lesson was suspended while the folks rolled in the pews with laughter.

The incident quickly spread around the small town "grapevine" and was obviously instrumental in giving birth to a conspiracy to get back at Father Ken. The next time he was coming back from the States, a whole group piled into a truck with the donkey and went to meet him at the airport. They decorated the animal with ribbons and hung a sign on both sides that said, "Welcome Back, Padre Ken. Have a nice trip to San Lucas." They tethered it just outside the entrance to the terminal and waited to get his reaction. It was predictable and well worth the trouble. He threw his head back and roared with laughter. Everyone rode back to the mission joking and laughing all the way.

We still have a donkey around the parish. No one uses it for serious work. However, neither Fathers Ken nor John need to feel bad. One Palm Sunday when the *burro* was borrowed to re-enact the entrance into Jerusalem this stubborn beast wouldn't even let the Lord himself mount and ride him.

Assault on Volcano Atitlán

To the west of San Lucas rise two majestic volcanos. The larger forms a distinctly pointed cone and at 11,650 feet it is the tallest mountain in the area. One reason to climb a mountain is just because it is there, but I have been to the peak of a few higher than this one and I remember the thrill. I wanted to experience again the illusion of being able to see forever and feel the satisfaction of just making it to the top.

December is the best month to climb because of the clear, dry weather. Some adventurous friends were coming for a visit after Christmas, so we planned the great assault.

As often happens, the best laid plans need revision. In this case, the problem was that Joe and Susan didn't come as scheduled. After the excitement and hype of Christmas, the wait was very difficult. I didn't know what had happened or if they would still come. I had been with them for three New Year's Eve celebrations in a row and was so looking forward to sharing with them the past year's events. That my Christmas mail had begun to arrive only made me more lonesome.

Just when I had given up hope, they came waltzing in. Suddenly all was better. Their luggage had gotten lost in Mexico City, and they had to either wait for it or buy a whole new wardrobe.

I had a marvelous time being a tour guide around the mission and catching up on the latest "news among friends." New Year's Eve was appropriately celebrated with refreshments, goodies, music and dancing out under the stars. But the conversation was never far from the climb that was slated for New Year's Day.

74

We planned a two-day assault. Though it is possible for experienced and conditioned athletes to do it in one day, prudence subdued our pride. We would go about three-quarters of the way up the first day, sleep out in the forest, then continue to the summit and return the next day.

With our two young Indian lads as guides, we started up the trail. The weather was clear and warm but that didn't make it easy for us middle-aged softies. The scenery was breath-taking and provided wonderful excuses for frequent stops. Our guides seemed amused as we wiped away the sweat and gasped for air.

My heavy duty hiking boots didn't quite fit and were tearing up my feet. Joe had not been feeling well and had the symptoms of intestinal parasites: diarrhea, high temperature, and low energy level. Sue was doing fine in spite of not being accustomed to the high altitude.

Dusk was near as we passed a clearing in the thick forest. Joe suggested that we stay, but I knew we still had a long way to go and urged them on. The steep trail wound through the towering pines and thick underbrush. We had to stop often for Joe. I carried his backpack to allow him to keep going but finally he said, "I cannot go any further."

We looked around for a place to roll out blankets and build a fire. There really was nothing adequate, but what else could we do? The combination of being sweaty from over-exertion and the settling in of the cool night air suddenly got to Joe. He was dangerously close to hypothermia: deeply chilled, nauseous, and listless. It can be a killer and we had to act fast.

We had brought nothing along with us to make a hot drink, but we wrapped him in a blanket and quickly built a fire. Still, he remained cold and unresponsive. I didn't know about Sue, but I was getting scared. I had already scrapped the idea of trying to reach the summit the next day. My only thought was to get Joe warm and off the mountain as quickly as possible.

Realizing that my sleeping bag was the warmest thing we had, I made Joe get in and snuggle close to the fire and to us. The place was not very comfortable—very inclined and bumpy, but it would have to do for the night. Finally he started to warm up a bit and his nausea went away. However, the sacrifice for me was terrific. I had to spend the night sharing a small blanket with his wife. And we all had to snuggle close to keep each other warm! I can laugh about it now, but at the time it didn't seem funny.

In the morning, our guides went on up the mountain while we turned tail and headed for home. The great assault was over and without any feeling of accomplishment or vision of new horizons. We were just a little wiser and felt a lot older.

The retreat was rich in the experience of meeting so many native folks trotting up to their cornfields to bring down the year's harvest. We could not imagine that walk with a hundred pounds of corn on our back. Some entire families with children about eight or ten years old were coming up. One man even offered us his lunch for the day. We must have looked as though we were ready to collapse. We did return safe and sore about noon.

Some day there may be another opportunity to conquer that peak, but for now I am content to have escaped with a few blisters and a story to tell.

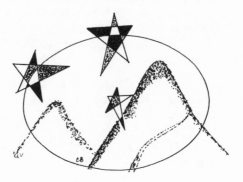

Time Out at Likin

My roots in rural Minnesota did not promote the appreciation of an ocean beach. We enjoyed the nearby lakes, and the story book image of skinny dipping down by the river was not foreign to us as young boys, but the sea was an unknown mystery. I first saw the ocean after graduating from high school and, since then, have been drawn back again and again to savor its gifts.

Two hours south of San Lucas, the powerful waves constantly reshape the Pacific coastline. Our mission staff decided to go there for a few days of rest. After loading the van with lots of towels, refreshments, and sun screen lotion, we headed for Likin.

Likin is (or was) a small recreational area situated on a long, narrow strip of land with the surf pounding in on one side and the quiet backwaters on the other. There were bungalows, a restaurant, hotel, two swimming pools (one with salt water and one fresh) and, most importantly, the charcoal gray sand beach.

As we were ferried through the winding, narrow backwaters, I remember being fascinated by the mangrove trees. They were like trees on stilts with their roots holding them six feet above the water at low tide. Then there were the little fish with four eyes (I swear it's true) that surfaced along the route, as if to check out who was invading their domain.

We chose the bungalows so that Father Greg could serve as cook and bottle washer and we could have some separate space, if we wanted, as well as some common places to gather. We were almost the only people in the whole complex. It was like having our own tropical island.

While Father Greg fussed with the food, Father Tom, a retired priest living with us at the mission, enjoyed his refreshments and reminiscings. Father John hibernated in his cave until the sun cooled or hid behind the clouds. The rest of us read, walked the beach, swam a few hours a day, played cards or just enjoyed the time to talk about all things important or trivial, personal or cosmic.

Just the memories of those days fill me with a sense of peace—the balm and rhythm of the sea, the cosmic awareness and union that it invites, and the solitude on the beach that seemed brimming with God's presence and the presence of all whom I love. I also saw the paradox of the timelessness of the natural rhythms alongside the ephemeral dreams of mortals, constructed of stone and mortar and "protected" by huge, cement retaining walls . . . many were already crumbling.

It is rare that I am moved to write poetry. But I felt the urge to write something of the mystery that I encountered on that beach.

Sea Dance

Like thunder, the cataracts curl constantly
then crash rhythmically upon sister sand.

She lies spread eagle,
every particle caressed,
trusting the eternal mystery of ebb and flow
of being lost and thus found.

And brother sea comes again and again
but gently, in the end,
presenting his gifts wrapped in flowing foam.

Clench-fisted the cemented guardians crumble and fall
while her supple curves stretch on endlessly.

Befriending the dragon of such power,
she lends her secret and her treasures
to all who tread her pregnant womb.

In the planting of the seed
surrender is the key,

offering without reserve,
yielding to the mystery.

And of this embrace what is born
but ecstasy in the very dancing,
and union with the All!

Likin is gone now; so are all the fortified beach homes that were sprinkled along the shore. They were victims of the high tides and the persistent pounding surf. What remains is an even more solitary beach full of mystery and wonderful memories.

"Surely you know that you are God's temple and that God's Spirit lives in you." (1 Cor. 3:16)

A Trip to Tikal

Non-business travel is foolishness to some, to others it is life's choicest portion . . . the opportunity to experience new cultures, places, and peoples. My friend, Virg, first planted in me the desire to visit Tikal, the ancient cultural center of the great Mayan civilization in northern Guatemala. Though not given to exhuberance, he went on and on in superlatives about the marvelous tombs and temples hidden in the Tikal jungle.

My first attempt to visit was a challenge to my patience and flexibility. The army was flying a shuttle back and forth to the ruins, but, apparently, only when it was most convenient for them. I waited with a group of friends for six hours. Finally, a funny looking machine that looked like a flying watermelon taxied up to the loading ramp. At this point, some of my companions were losing enthusiasm for the trip. The sight of this alleged airplane turned mere frustration to full blown anxiety. So when the plane filled up and we were still outside we said, "Forget it!" and, instead, went out to eat.

A year later, Father John Brandis, a priest on a sabbatical, came to San Lucas, and we decided to explore Tikal together. Perhaps the best way I can communicate some impressions and discoveries of that adventure would be to share a portion of my personal journal written on site.

". . . I want to express something of what another culture, another group of people has stirred in me through the ruins of their capital, left behind in a steaming jungle. Unfortunately, words seem incapable of capturing and transferring the experience in any way; I should paint a picture, chisel a stone or erect an altar.

80

"What a mystery! I keep wanting to be transported in time, even for a few moments, back to the full flower of the Classic Mayan Tikal. The values expressed in architecture, ceremony and tombs seem incomprehensible in detail but still deeply moving because of the scope of what is here. We had a great guide who was able to help us understand some of the hidden marvels of this abandoned culture.

"Today is the Feast of the Dedication of St. John Lateran. Usually I feel a little cheated when the feast supercedes the normal Sunday celebration, but today it seemed appropriate for us as we celebrated the God-life within our own temple (Mass) while we sat upon the high, 1200-year-old Temple of Inscriptions. It was a Mayan ceremonial temple that included occasional human sacrifice.

"It sits in the midst of tens of thousands of temples, altars, and other sacred places. The air is full of stories ready to be told about how they were built, how the Mayans celebrated, and how they died. . . great exploits and strange rituals that saw it a great privilege to be sacrificed.

"The human blood-letting seems very strange, but when I think of the Christian story that I, as priest, relive in a special way 'most every day when I say, "This is my body. . . my blood, given for you," I have to admit that their practices were not so strange or different as to be totally beyond comprehension.

"Today as I looked past the elements of the sacrifice of Jesus, I could see below the altar on which someone felt privileged to be offered as a sacrifice to the gods that they reverenced. What is the difference and what is the unity between those two actions and the cultures that gave them birth? Somehow I feel that the differences are as equally profound as the unity between them.

"Here are some of the prayers provided today by the Church as we strolled among the ancient sacred temples in the Holy City of Tikal.

'God, our Father, from living stones, your chosen
people, you built an eternal temple to your glory.
Increase the spiritual gifts you have given to
your Church so that your people may continue to grow
into the new and eternal Jerusalem.'
(Opening prayer from the *Roman Missal* for the
Feast of the Dedication of St. John Lateran.)

'I have chosen and sanctified this house, says the Lord,
that my name may remain in it for all time.'
(Alleluia Verse)

'Like living stones let yourself be built on Christ as a
spiritual house, a holy priesthood.' "
(Communion Antiphon)

Father John and I enjoyed immensely our trip to Tikal. The
whole experience was a source of inspiration and a fountain of
prayer and reflection for many days. As with many incidents of
travel, this story has no clear ending. To the born traveler there
is always another mystery to be encountered just out of sight
around the bend.

An International Dinner Party

The old fashioned dinner party—the inviting of friends and neighbors over for the sheer pleasure of a good home cooked meal and stimulating conversation—has gone out of style, they say. It's a diminishing art form that is being neglected in favor of cheap entertainment on television, or the easy-out of eating in restaurants. Whatever the reason for its demise, I'd like to call it back by the sharing of a story about a special international dinner party.

Our hostess was the gracious and delightful Kiyomi. She is a Japanese United Nations Children's Fund (UNICEF) worker. I got to know her because she was the only other person in language school that was a tennis buff. We would play once or twice a week when we needed a diversion from the intense mental concentration of language study. It was also a relief to speak with someone in English. She was fluent in English because she had studied in the States and had lived in New York before taking her assignment in Guatemala.

Though we came from completely different worlds, with different family and religious backgrounds, I found her interested in the work of the mission and eager to experience more of the religiously charged customs of the Indian culture. I invited her to come to San Lucas for Holy Week. She absorbed everything with excitement and appreciation. She even went on a picnic and swam with one hundred and twenty kids from the orphanage. That takes great courage and stamina.

We enjoyed her visit. In her generous manner, she extended an invitation for us to visit her apartment in the Capital. We accepted immediately, though we were not sure it would ever really happen.

83

But it did. One Friday, Sister Linda Wanner and I had gone into the big city for shopping and decided to call Kiyomi to see what she was doing. She had planned a dinner party that night and though it was short notice, insisted that we come too.

We didn't anticipate the rich diversity of cultures and people that would share this delicious Japanese meal. Through her work with UNICEF, Kiyomi met people from all over the world. The nine guests were born in or came from ten different countries of Europe, North and Latin America and the Far East. Each spoke an average of three languages. Sister Linda and I were self-conscious of our limited education as mere bilinguals. We were grateful that English was the common language that everyone knew fluently.

The food and hospitality were excellent, but the most interesting part of the evening was the comparing of different cultural values, ways of expressing oneself, political and legal structures. What a difference there is in the human family! For example, one man from Korea talked about the value of ancestral heritage in his culture. He could trace his lineage back forty-five generations to the seventh century whereas I barely know the names of my grandparents who died before I was born!

Kiyomi talked of how the Japanese use three different verb expressions depending on whether one is speaking to a respected elder, a peer or a child. I also learned from her that the oriental system of writing, that uses symbols not associated with specific sounds, allows the Japanese and Chinese to read each other's newspapers although they cannot understand each others' spoken word.

Another fascinating topic was the various legal systems. North American and Western European systems presume a person's innocence until proven guilty but in many other countries, including Guatemala, the burden of proof is on the accused. This can lead to terrible corruption of judges and lawyers as innocent persons without proof often feel bribery is justified to gain their freedom.

The evening was too short to contain all we wanted to talk about. I wished we could get together every week and call it "Kiyomi's International School of Cooking and Culture." I felt sad that, because of ignorance and fears, many people distrust what is different from their own values and point of view. I hoped that more of these dinners could be shared by more people. It certainly would help break down the prejudice and hostilities that keep people apart.

A Gift of Thanks

The question was: "What would be a fitting thank you gift from the people of San Lucas to the Diocese of New Ulm, Minnesota, for the support in money, prayer, and personnel over the last twenty-five years?" Pondering this question led Father Greg to the dream of a super-sculpture of what is sacred and a sign of life to this people of Mayan roots, that is, corn.

The Mayan story of creation reveals that the Creator Gods first attempted to make human beings of mud, then of wood. These efforts failed; the mud was too soft and dissolved in water whereas the people of wood were destroyed because they did not remember their creators and give thanks.

Finally, Grandmother God shaped the first human beings from the fruit of this sacred plant and breathed into them the life-breath of the spirit. The beings recognized their Creator and gave thanks. The substance from which they were created was cornmeal from the sacred plant, *maiz* or corn (from *Popol Vuh,* the collection of ancient Mayan writings). [7]

A woodcarver, who is also the clinic's medical doctor, Dr. Miza, agreed to create the work of art: three standing stalks of corn each with its ripening ear, with the vines and fruit of squash and climbing beans woven around the base of the sculpture and up the stalk. All would be carved from one solid log of cedar measuring twelve feet long and two and one-half feet square.

The five-thousand-pound log was hauled up from the coast by truck, then dragged into Dr. Miza's house by twenty men. Over the next six months, the artist and his assistant, Luis, eagerly shaped the huge trunk. Little by little emerged the stalks of corn—the plant most significant in the life and sustenance of the Mayan people. While the creation process continued, many of the townspeople would come to watch with joy and awe as the wood was transformed before their eyes.

Father Greg and the carvers were especially pleased to see the looks of admiration and surprise on the faces of the professional movers employed to pack and ship the sculpture. They were accustomed to moving extraordinary objects, but were truly impressed by the magnitude and rare quality of this work. They took great care in moving it to various locations in the village for photographers. Small crowds gathered at each place, and had the camera been turned around the film would have captured expressions containing a mixture of curiosity, wonderment and proud satisfaction.

From San Lucas, the sculpture first traveled to the National Center for Tourism (INGUAT) in Guatemala City for a week's exposition. The dream continued to unfold as the occasion was enhanced by music, food and native arts and crafts—all in an effort to promote the creative talents of the rural Guatemalan people who are so often unappreciated and even belittled.

After repacking, the gift was sent to New Ulm, where it was presented to the people of the diocese. The celebration of thanksgiving included a Mass, a turkey dinner for four hundred people cooked by local Guatemalans, and the customary words of thanks and counter-thanks.

If I had not been there—been a part of the story of this corn statue almost from the beginning—I could remain untouched by it or objectively judge it as no more than an excellent promotional idea. But I would be denying the power of art to contain and express what is in the human heart. I would be denying the artist in me. . . that part that can transform matter into meaning. For I saw the hands shaping the wood (the same skilled hands that help heal me when I am sick) and I saw hundreds of glistening eyes gazing in awe.

More than anything, I know that the words written for the statue's presentation by the Guatemalan, Carlos Jacinto, come from the heart:

> "Thanks for that generous and tiring help you have unstintingly provided to bring out the best that is in us. Thanks to these material and moral resources, our community and many others have seen remarkable progress in the fields of culture, education, religion, economy—the fruit of long and untiring years of mutual and hard work. For this reason, in the very heart of this Sculpture is locked our affection and our love for you. In a word, *NIMALAJ MALTIOX CHIWE*". Many thanks and God Bless You."

Epilogue

My love of the people in these stories urges me to share the mission statement that gives direction to our efforts at San Lucas and helps us set priorities.

Mission Statement of San Lucas Tolimán

As disciples of the Lord, open to the movement of the Spirit, we are called to promote the kingdom of God as a viable option for the people of San Lucas.

Based on the life of Jesus, revealed in the Scriptures and reflected in the inherent spirituality of the people, we seek to facilitate each person's and each community's spiritual journey through the celebration of the sacraments and a life of mutual service.

As Jesus responded to the people and their needs, we believe it is our mission also to respond to the expressed, felt needs of the people of San Lucas and of the surrounding areas that form the larger community. In our response we include the individuals with specific needs who come to the mission seeking help. Our purpose is to deal with both the immediate effects of poverty and their root causes.

Recognizing that all of us are made in the image and likeness of God, our goal is to enhance and enrich the whole person. Thus, we promote the *dignity, self-respect,* and *development* of the people we have been called to serve. This is a step by step process which shows itself in educational, medical, nutritional, spiritual, and socio-economic planning and programs.

As a cross-cultural parish we are aware of the rich heritage of the Guatemalan people and recognize that the process of ongoing conversion for all of us is facilitated by the mutual sharing of cultural values and spiritual insights. Thus we recognize that we are called to be a bridge, to share with our brothers and sisters in the United States of America who have been associated with our mission, either as members of the New Ulm Diocese or as benefactors, by offering hospitality and by sharing the culture, struggles, hopes and aspirations of the people of Guatemala.

Within our mission we constantly seek alternative ways of peace and justice that are based on the interdependence of people who share their gifts and resources in an atmosphere of Christian love.

If you would like to contribute in any way to the support of the San Lucas Mission in the spirit of this statement write to:

San Lucas Mission Office
1400 Sixth North Street
New Ulm, MN 56073

Endnotes

1. I am indebted to Dr. Carlos Gehlert Mata for the facts and observations in this section. They were offered in a speech given in San Lucas Tolimán on February 25, 1987. Dr. Mata is the present Minister of Health in Guatemala (1989).

2. Ibid.

3. Diocese of Sololá, *Plan Pastoral 1989-1990,* published in 1989.

4. Mata, Dr. Carlos Gehlert.

5. Couderc, Saint Theresa, quoted from a letter to Mother de Larochenegly, r.c., then Superior General of the congregation, August 10, 1866. The letter can be found in the uncopyrighted book, *Congregation of Our Lady of the Retreat in the Cenacle: Anthology of Congregation Documents,* p. 178. Translated by Mary Louise Moore, r.c., 1984.

6. The speech was quoted on a calendar without a source given. Research indicates that the often quoted words have not been authenticated. Cf. "Thus Spoke Chief Seattle: The Story of an Undocumented Speech," by Jerry L. Clark, in *Prologue* (Vol. 17, No. 1, 1985, pp. 58-65).

7. *Popul Wuh,* Ancient Stories of the Quiche Indians of Guatemala. Adaptation, notes, vocabulary and English version by Albertina Saravia E., ©1980. Published by Editorial Piedra Santa, Guatemala, C.A. Title in Spanish, *Popol Wuh;* Antiguas historias de los indios quichés de Guatemala, ©1965, Albertina Saravia E., Ed. PORRUA HNOS., Mexico.